HUNTRESS INITIATE

HUNTRESS INITIATE

HUNTRESS CLAN SAGA™ BOOK 1

JAMIE DAVIS

DISRUPTIVE IMAGINATION

Copyright © 2019 Jamie Davis
Cover copyright © LMBPN Publishing

LMBPN Publishing
PMB 196, 2540 South Maryland Pkwy
Las Vegas, NV 89109

First US Edition, November 2019
eBook ISBN: 978-1-64202-603-0
Print ISBN: 978-1-64202-604-7

THE HUNTRESS INITIATE TEAM

Thanks to the Beta Readers
John Ashmore, Kelly O'Donnell, Sarah Weir, Mary Morris,
Larry Omans

Thanks to the JIT Readers

Dorothy Lloyd
Jeff Eaton
Diane L. Smith
Dave Hicks
Peter Manis
Deb Mader

If I've missed anyone, please let me know!

Editor
The Skyhunter Editing Team

"If we don't leave her, they'll kill her along with the rest of us."

Naomi checked the rearview mirror for the tenth time in the last minute.

They were close.

She could feel it.

The amulet's warning was never wrong, and the intense cold coming off it sent a chill through her again.

Brian, Naomi's husband, shook his head. "That makes no sense. You've got power and abilities. You explained it to me after we got married. You've protected us and kept us hidden this long. Can't you just—"

"Don't you see? After everything I did, they still found us. I'm telling you, someone betrayed the clan from within. They're all gone. Nothing I've done has stopped the killing. Trust me when I say we're screwed. I can't protect her or us anymore. The witch told us the coven's spell would only hide us long enough to have the baby. It was only temporary. The protection has faded."

"But giving her up this way?"

"You think I like this? You think this is easy for me? This is the only way. Even then, it may not be enough."

Naomi spun the wheel, turning at the last second onto a side street as she raced through the early morning streets of Baltimore. She glanced in the mirror, watching to see if anyone followed them from their original path.

"Look, Brian. There's a slim chance I can break whatever tracking spell they have on us, but if I can't, there's only one way this will end. I'm sorry to bring you into this. You didn't understand what it meant to marry into a hunter clan. I see now my father was right. It wasn't fair."

"I'm not sorry. I want to make sure we're not abandoning our baby when there's a chance you can still work it out."

Naomi shook her head. "I can't take that kind of chance with her life. No one has been able to stop the assassins yet. Hunters far better than me have tried and failed."

Brian glanced back at the baby in the carrier buckled to the middle of the back seat. "Where are you going to leave her? You're not going to knock on some door and leave her on the front steps with a note, are you?"

"Something like that."

Naomi spotted her destination ahead. The blue light over the garage doors spilled a muted light over the sidewalk in front of the old brick firehouse. Some of her ancestors had worked as firefighters here in the city. A few of these older firehouses had protection circles that still held residual power. It might be enough to keep the baby safe.

A last check in the mirror showed a clear street behind them. Nodding more to convince herself than Brian,

Naomi pulled over and stopped at the curb in front of the old building.

"Get her car seat out of the back. I'll write a quick note."

"Naomi, are you—"

"Sure? Yes, now hurry. We've lost our pursuit, but they're still close. I can feel them coming."

A fresh chill emanating from the amulet punctuated her dire prediction.

Flipping open the glove box, Naomi dug for a pen and a scrap of paper. She pulled out the broken stub of a dull pencil and an empty bank envelope.

It would have to do.

She scribbled a brief note, re-read it, and nodded again, climbing out of the car to join Brian in the splash of the headlights on the sidewalk.

Her husband's grief-stricken face tugged at her heart. It almost made her doubt her decision. She shook it off, though.

"Give her to me and get back in the car. I'll be right there."

Brian hesitated for a moment before handing over the infant carrier.

Naomi took it and stared down at her beautiful daughter, barely a week old. She blinked away a few tears and walked up to the firehouse personnel door, off to one side of the vehicle ramp.

She set the carrier down. Kneeling beside it. Naomi reached up behind her neck, unclasping the silver chain that held the hunter amulet she'd received on the day of her initiation. It had never failed her. Perhaps it would serve her daughter as well, even though she'd never know its true powers.

Naomi slid amulet and chain into the bank envelope and fumbled with the pencil stub as she added another two lines to the note. She placed it on the blanket covering her daughter.

Squealing tires in the distance somewhere up the street behind her alerted Naomi to potential pursuit. Her hand brushed her chest where the cold chill of the protection amulet used to rest.

The sound from the approaching vehicle wasn't a coincidence. As soon as she'd removed the hunter's amulet, its inherent protection around her had dissipated. She had to leave before it was too late to save at least the baby.

Naomi pressed the door buzzer for a long second, then raced back to the car. She put it in gear and drove away, reaching over to squeeze her husband's hand as they left their daughter in the darkness behind them.

Two cars with black-tinted windows raced past the firehouse a few seconds later, oblivious to the baby carrier on the sidewalk next to the entrance.

A minute after the two cars passed by, the firehouse personnel door opened. A young man in the uniform of the Baltimore Fire Department stepped out to see who'd rung the buzzer.

"Anyone there, McKinley?" the lieutenant asked from inside.

"You're not going to believe this, sir. It's a baby."

"Damn, not again. I've got too much paperwork to do as it is. Is there any identification?"

McKinley bent down and picked up the carrier. "Just this."

He handed the lieutenant the envelope with the hand-scrawled note.

Her name is Quinn.
Give her the necklace.
It is her birthright.

McKinley checked the empty street one last time, then stepped inside with the baby and closed the door.

CHAPTER ONE

"Quinn, hurry up. We can't be late on our first real shift at the testing center. They'll fire us."

Quinn frowned. Her roommate's anxiety about things like this was typical. That was just the way Taylor was. Quinn preferred to take things as they came, without anyone else's drama.

Taylor's anxiety about the job was understandable. As a total computer nerd, getting a job testing software at a company like VirSync was a dream come true.

Despite the differences between the two of them, she'd been Quinn's best friend for most of high school, becoming close after Taylor had helped her when Quinn spent a portion of her eighth-grade year homeless on the streets of Baltimore. It was either the street or staying in an abusive foster care situation.

Eventually, child protective services placed her in a new and more stable home situation. She and Taylor had remained friends, though. In some ways, Quinn believed she owed the other girl her life. Something deep inside told Quinn that was important.

"Chill, Taylor. I'll be right there."

As Quinn shrugged into her t-shirt, her hand brushed her lucky pendant. It was the only thing she had from her birth mother. It had been left with her as a baby at a fire-house door eighteen years before. The child and the pendant on a silver chain came with a note stating Quinn's name.

She tucked it inside her t-shirt's collar, tracing the outline of it beneath the fabric. It might be her imagination at work, but Quinn had grown up believing the small silver oval somehow warned her when something was wrong.

Quinn grinned as she rubbed her thumb over the surface, turning it over through the fabric. The pendant was inscribed with a stylized tree on one side and what one of her teachers had once described as some sort of Germanic runes on the other.

She smiled as she pulled on her jeans. The pendant's magical protections were just another part of the child-hood daydreams she had to put behind her now that she had graduated. All those times she'd imagined the charm warning her of trouble were a product of an overactive child's imagination. Quinn knew she'd just been lucky, and prepared to act on that luck.

She'd grown up believing in her ability to recognize dangerous situations facing her, like her foster-father's approach from behind that night so long ago. It had allowed her to escape him, and she'd run away to the rela-tive safety of the streets.

"Quinn, come on." Taylor popped her head into the open doorway, her long blonde ponytail bouncing behind her. "We don't want to be late. We get our first VR test assignments today."

"I'm coming, I'm coming. You heard the instructors in the orientation sessions. Everyone gets the same sort of assignments to start. Only after we go through a few VR sessions in the testing system will we get segmented into different groups based on ability."

"Well, I'm not taking any chances. You know how lucky we were to get this job right out of high school the way we did. It's the only way we can afford to share this apartment."

Quinn shook her head as Taylor disappeared back into the living room. Despite Taylor's early enthusiasm for the job, Quinn still wasn't sold on everything it promised.

Quinn had been recruited by her lacrosse coach right after the graduation ceremonies. She'd directed Quinn to a link online, recommending she apply. The coach had told her the job was perfect for an athlete like her. Knowing Taylor would want to be included in the opportunity to work for the Baltimore-based gaming software company, Quinn had shared the link with her best friend.

They'd applied together and had both been both offered probationary spots in the new test program for VirSync.

Quinn figured she'd try the new job, at least for now. The money was too good to turn down, and she needed a place to stay now that she was officially out from under the state's care.

She and Taylor had dreamed of getting an apartment

together after leaving school. It was hard to turn the opportunity down when the VirSync recruiter told them the job offer included an apartment for the two of them. It was better than most places Quinn had known growing up, and there was no way she could turn it down.

Quinn shoved a change of clothes and a towel in the duffel bag as directed by their orientation instructions for VR testing days. They'd each change at work into a specially-designed black bodysuit. Each had been fitted for one during their orientation sessions.

Taylor poked her head back into the room. She rolled her eyes and said, "You don't even have your shoes on. Quinn, please! We're going to be late."

"I know. This job is important for both of us. Go get ready, and I'll meet you outside at the Jeep."

Quinn smiled as Taylor gave an exasperated grunt and left again. They were opposites in so many ways, but that seemed to help them get along, since they had complementary skills.

Taylor, although most thought her a typical absent-minded computer nerd-type, had gravitated to sports in high school and joined her friend Quinn on the lacrosse team, surprising many with her athleticism.

Dark-haired, athletic Quinn had never liked tech much, preferring to focus on athletic training, and eventually on various martial arts programs offered by the city over the years.

Taylor had often remarked that while she was the brains of the duo, Quinn, with her natural street smarts and wisdom, was the heart.

Quinn slid on her sneakers and shouldered her gym

bag. She headed for the door, stopped to make sure it would lock behind her, and went downstairs to where Taylor waited by the Jeep.

As she left the newly renovated apartment building, she looked back at the three-story structure and shook her head. Who gave eighteen-year-olds their own apartment as part of any compensation package? It didn't make sense.

"Quinn, hurry up."

Taylor stood next to Quinn's beat-up Jeep Wrangler, her most prized possession. She'd scrimped and saved to afford it, and even though the pay from the new job could have let her buy her a better model, Quinn was happy with this one for now.

She unlocked the passenger door as she passed it. Taylor smiled and climbed in.

Quinn got in the driver's seat and started the engine. She settled the faded Baltimore Orioles ball cap she'd grabbed from the dashboard on her close-cropped brunette hair and turned to Taylor. "See, we're leaving on time. You just have to have a little faith."

"Quinn, it's always best to be early. You remember what Miss Hudson used to say in school. Early is on time and on time is late."

Quinn shook her head. "Hey, we've graduated. We don't have to listen to teachers anymore."

Taylor laughed. "It's just a good thing to do. I know if this was a sporting event or a sparring match, you'd be there an hour early to do extra warm-ups before anyone else arrived. This is a great job. It's okay to like it, even though you didn't want to take it at first."

"That's not the whole reason. It's strange how this job

fell in our laps the way it did. Don't you wonder how they even knew to get coach to offer it to me?"

Taylor dismissed that with a wave of her hand. "It was probably one of the guidance counselors trying to do us a favor. You know how they were always going on about how they were there to help us, especially with you growing up in the system the way you did. We shouldn't be disrespectful when something good is handed to us."

"I'm not disrespecting the offer, Taylor. I just want to understand what is happening. They're paying us a lot of money to do...what? Play a video game?"

"You heard the recruiter when we went to the interview," Taylor replied. "It's so much more than just a game. It could change the way they train our nation's soldiers forever. They wanted people who were active and athletic to try it because of the physical demands of the system. We both like video games, and we are both athletes. As far as I'm concerned, it's the perfect job."

Quinn drove on as Taylor continued to outline all the reasons this was a good idea. Quinn decided to put her concerns in the back of her mind and focus on getting to work on time. She got on the Beltway that circled the city and started around it to the exit that led to the company's office complex. She had to hurry through afternoon rush hour traffic to get there before six o'clock. Quinn didn't want to hear Taylor tell her "I told you so."

Despite Taylor's concerns about being late, they arrived ten minutes before their proposed start time that evening. Quinn stopped at the gate to flash her badge at the card reader.

Inside the small guard shack, the armed, uniformed security guard stared at his monitor for a few seconds, then looked up, smiled, and waved them through. Quinn waited until the iron gate slid aside far enough for her to go through, then drove into the lot and headed toward the employee parking area.

As they passed the guard shack, Taylor waved at the security guard. "He's kind of cute."

Quinn groaned. "Taylor, it's our first day outside of orientation. Let's not start a hot office romance on day one, okay?"

"I was just telling you he was cute. He was checking you out, and you didn't even look in his direction."

"I could see him fine. I'm just not looking for anybody right now. I want to get on with my life. I don't need any romantic encumbrances."

Taylor let out an exasperated sigh. "Quinn, you're the only eighteen-year-old I know who thinks getting tangled up in romantic encumbrances is a problem. Loosen up, girlfriend. Who knows, you might meet the person of your dreams in there. There were more than a few likely prospects in our small orientation group, and we get to meet others we don't know today."

Quinn smiled as she pulled into a parking spot a few rows from the front entrance. Taylor had always tried to be a good wingwoman. While she was shy, Taylor was positively brazen when it came to finding Quinn dates.

At first, Quinn had gone along with the fun, but she found it difficult to get close to anyone beyond some limited one-night stands. She trusted only a few people in the world enough to let her guard down. So far, no random teenage girl or guy had been able to qualify, and she was fine with that.

There were a bunch of other people their age congregating in the parking lot. She saw at least ten, including three or four she didn't recognize.

It was easy to pick the test candidates out of the crowd of older office workers exiting the building at the end of their normal workday. All the young folks were heading in while the oldies all came out.

Quinn clipped the new ID badge on her t-shirt collar and turned off the Jeep. "Come on, Taylor. You don't want to be late."

They laughed at the role reversal as the two of them hopped out and started toward the front of the building.

Taylor gave Quinn a playful shove as they walked along the sidewalk. "Quinn Faust, one of these days, your snark is going to catch up with you. I want to be there when it does."

Quinn shot her best friend a half-grin as they reached the front doors. A tall blond guy about their age saw them coming and waited to hold the door for them as they got there. Taylor smiled at him and nodded to thank him. Quinn murmured her thanks and headed in after Taylor.

The guy followed them in, speeding up until he caught up with them halfway across the expansive lobby. "You both are here for the VR job too, right?"

Quinn remembered the orientation briefing on the secrecy surrounding the project and said nothing.

Taylor either forgot the rules or ignored them and jumped in with an answer right away. "Yeah, are you?"

The guy nodded. "I'm Fergus, Fergus Bishop."

"I'm Taylor. Taylor Haney. You should meet my best friend here, Quinn Faust."

"It's nice to meet you. I wasn't sure I was going to like this job. I generally don't like meeting new people, but you both seem all right."

Quinn shot him a glance. "Careful, we could be ax murderers."

Fergus started to laugh, then stopped as he caught Quinn's deadly-serious stare.

"Quinn, stop that," Taylor said. "Don't pay any attention to her. That's her typical poor attempt at humor."

Quinn's stern expression broke into a broad grin. This guy was gullible enough. Probably more muscles than brains.

She and Taylor turned back to the front as they finished crossing the foyer. A woman sat in a business suit behind a counter, her brown hair pulled back into a bun. Her name tag read Elizabeth. She had just directed several other people their age toward the double doors to the right.

"Are you three checking in for the test center?"

"Yeah," Quinn said. She glanced to the right, where the others had gone. They hadn't been to that wing before. All their orientation sessions and interviews had been in the central part of office building. "I guess we follow those other kids?"

The woman smiled. "You've got it. Just follow them down the long hallway. There's a bright red line painted on the floor, which will take you back to the secure testing facility. You have your badges with you, right?"

The three of them nodded.

"Good. Don't ever forget them since you'll need them to enter the testing facility when you get back there. Most people who work here don't have access to it."

Quinn smiled. "Thank you. We'll remember." She led the way, with Taylor and Fergus falling in behind her, pulled open the right-hand door, and walked through into a broad hallway with white linoleum floors.

Sure enough, a broad red stripe ran down the center. Blue and green stripes paralleled it. The blue stripe continued all the way down the corridor with the red one. The green line peeled off to the left, stopping at a set of doors labeled Chemical Receiving.

The red line followed the blue one a little farther, then turned right, heading through a pair of sealed doors with a sign marked Research Candidate Testing.

Quinn glanced at the blue line before turning to the left at the far end. She wondered what it led to.

"Are you coming, Quinn?" Taylor asked.

Quinn realized she'd pulled out her pendant and had been rubbing it between her thumb and forefinger as she stared down the hall. The small silver charm felt cold to the touch.

She tucked it back into her shirt as she turned to Taylor and smiled. "I'm coming, I'm coming. This place is just so big. It makes you wonder where all these corridors go to."

Taylor shrugged. "I guess we'll find out soon enough." She took her badge out and held it in front of the sensor next to the entrance.

The doors clicked open and receded into their respective walls for all three of them to enter a large room with several desks. Each had a computer keyboard and monitor built into it. Banks of electronics and blinking LED lights and dials covered one wall.

As they entered, a woman looked up from where she sat at a plain metal desk. "Let me see your badges, please."

Each of them held out their ID in turn, Quinn going last.

The woman checked the screen in front of her for each badge, then told them, "Head through the far doors and go down the hall until you get to the locker rooms. There's one for men and one for women. Your names are on your lockers. Leave your personal stuff from your duffel bag there and change into the custom VR jumpsuits you'll find hanging inside."

All three nodded and walked across the room to the indicated doors, which opened into another hallway. There were no lines on the plain white floor here. There was no need since there was only one way to go. On the righthand wall was a series of numbered doors. They started at one and continued down the long corridor. Quinn guessed there must be at least twenty doors.

Halfway down the hall were two doors on the left side, clearly marked men's and women's locker rooms.

The three of them separated. The two girls headed into the women's locker room, and Fergus pushed open the other door and went into the men's locker room next to it.

As she entered the noisy room, Quinn realized she hadn't worried about her reservations about the job since they'd entered the lobby. Nothing but excitement filled her now.

She smiled at Taylor, and her roomie returned the smile with a nod. They were about to see for the first time what their orientation instructor had called the next generation in computer-simulated training. While Quinn didn't have any idea what that meant, she was excited to find out.

CHAPTER TWO

Quinn and Taylor exited the locker room together a few minutes later, each dressed in a skintight charcoal-gray bodysuit with matching gray socks. The bottoms of the socks had rubberized tread to give them traction on the tile floor.

She glanced to her left, taking in Taylor's form-fitting outfit. She caught Taylor looking her way.

Both girls giggled.

"Pretty cool get-up, huh?" Quinn asked.

"Looking sharp," Taylor replied.

A group of VirSync employees dressed in matching khaki pants and polo shirts stood in the hall nearby. As the two came out of the locker room, four people separated from the group and moved toward them.

A man with lightly graying black hair stepped forward. He pointed at Quinn. "Quinn Faust?"

"That's me."

"I'm Phillip Ruiz." He hooked the finger over his shoulder at the short, red-haired woman standing behind him. "This is Velma Griffin. We'll be working with you during your testing. Come with us."

Quinn nodded and turned to follow them down the hallway, glancing over her shoulder at Taylor. She'd matched up with the other pair of handlers. Taylor looked back and smiled as she was led in the opposite direction.

"Faust, are you paying attention?" Phillip snapped.

"Yes, sir. Sorry, sir. What did you say?"

"I'm your system administrator. I handle your specific testing projects for the company. Velma, here, is your test program coordinator. She's the one who will be arranging your individual VR rig to get the most out of your specific talents and abilities while you're inside the training system."

Velma kept her eyes forward, only glancing in Quinn's direction once when her name was mentioned. She had yet to smile or exhibit any sort of expression. It all seemed sort of serious for an initial VR training session.

They continued a little way down the hall before stopping outside a door with a small laminated plaque on the wall next to it that said Test Room 8.

Phillip opened the door and then gestured for Velma and Quinn to enter. They walked into a small, square room about ten feet across. On the opposite wall was a fair-sized glass window with a gray metal door next to it.

A large counter and desk covered in computer monitors and electronic equipment jutted out in an L-shape beneath the window. The layout impressed Quinn.

Unsure what to do or say, Quinn nodded and said, "Nice layout."

Velma didn't acknowledge the comment as she sat

down and swiveled in her chair to face Quinn and Phillip. "I'll be monitoring your progress in the test scenario from here and making slight changes as we go along to dial in the system for your specific needs while inside the VR environment. The goal of our testing program is to make this system intuitive enough to adapt itself to any subject placed into it without outside support."

"Sounds good," Quinn said. "So, where do I go from here?"

"Through that door," Phillip said as Velma turned back to her monitors and started tapping on the keyboard in front of her.

He opened the gray door beside the window and waited for Quinn to enter ahead of him.

A darkened room lay on the far side. The faint hum of electronics filled the whole space with a tangible vibration that made the hairs on Quinn's arm to stand up.

A flash of cold against her breastbone reminded her of the hidden pendant beneath her bodysuit. She was supposed to have taken off all jewelry, but Quinn never took off the only token remaining from her parents.

Her hand drifted absently up to rest two fingers against the outline of the silver oval beneath the thin, flexible fabric. The chill passed through the skintight suit to her fingertips.

Quinn scanned the room. Her superstitious mind looked for some sort of threat, remembering the pendant's strange properties from her childhood and its seeming ability to predict bad things.

She shook her head. There was no one in the room but Phillip and her. On the wall opposite the window was a reclining examination couch. It was sort of like what Quinn imagined one would find in an upscale doctor's office.

At the head of the couch was a bank of floor-to-ceiling metal cabinets with rack-mounted computer systems and other electronics. All of the gear was ready to operate, indicated by the lights of various colors that flashed on various systems.

Quinn walked over to the couch and sat down, then looked back at Phillip. The orientation classes had prepared her for some of what was to come.

The whole testing system had been set up as a sort of virtual-reality video game. To make it palatable to players of military recruiting age, it had a modern fantasy aspect that included various mythical monsters like werewolves and vampires, among other things.

Quinn and the other testers in the system were tasked with hunting down the monsters and killing them. Those who were successful would be rewarded. Those who were not would be reevaluated as to whether they should remain in the system. The orientation class had been very clear that mission failure in the VR would not be tolerated and might be cause for dismissal.

Phillip smiled and walked over to her. He lifted a circular metal band with wires coming off it. The wires gathered into a bundle, and the harness stretched over to connect to different sections of the bank of electronics nearby.

Attached to the band was a visor-like set of goggles. This was the headgear used to enter the VR system.

Quinn nodded and reached out.

Phillip handed her the headset. "I'll help you get situated today, but you'll be expected to get yourself ready for insertion into the system in the future. Got it?"

Quinn nodded. She lifted the headgear and settled it over her head. It fit snuggly, resting just above her eyebrows. It was heavier than she expected, the weight of the harness pulling her head back if she didn't resist it.

Phillip made a few adjustments and tightened the band a little, then said, "Lie down and get comfortable."

He turned to the window into the outer room. "How's the connection, Velma? Are you getting good readings?"

Velma's tinny, amplified voice sounded over the speakers in the ceiling. "It's adequate. The system will adjust to keep it within normal parameters. We can begin the induction process."

Phillip nodded and headed to the door, pulling it shut behind him as he left.

Alone in the relative silence, Quinn laid down, feeling the vibration of the humming electronics along the wall nearby transmitted through the metal frame of the exam couch.

She took a deep breath and reached up to adjust the visor across her forehead and over her eyes, then waited for what came next. The orientation had said it would be just like falling asleep.

It wasn't.

A stabbing pain lanced through her head, matched by a burning chill on her chest, which Quinn's instantly foggy mind distantly realized came from her pendant. She blinked away tears as a light brighter than the sun seared her eyes within the visor.

Quinn started to cry out for help. Something must have gone wrong.

She didn't hear her voice. The system had somehow paralyzed her. She couldn't speak or move.

The combination of pain and light overwhelmed her senses, and everything faded into blackness. The last thing that passed through her awareness was a distant voice that sounded like Velma's chanting. The words made no sense and were in no language she recognized.

She struggled to remain awake and listen to the voice, trying to understand the words. In the end, she failed.

Darkness overwhelmed her.

CHAPTER THREE

Quinn's eyes fluttered open as she tried to orient herself. The sounds and cool, swirling air against her face made it clear she wasn't in the testing room anymore. Quinn looked up from where she stood on the sidewalk of a quiet downtown street. Despite the bright city lights, she could make out a few stars overhead as she stared upward.

Looking left and right on the vacant street corner, Quinn took in the rich textures and detail woven into the system. It all looked so real.

Hell, it *felt* real.

Quinn touched her cheek as the breeze picked up. If she didn't know better, she'd swear there was nothing virtual about it.

The street might have been somewhere nearby in downtown Baltimore, based on the style of the buildings in either direction. Two- and three-story row homes lined the street on both sides, with occasional shops scattered here and there.

On the opposite side of the street from Quinn sat a small grocery store. The light from the plastic sign suspended on a pole jutting out over the entrance, along with the interior lights, spilled a glow onto the sidewalk outside, just like a dozen similar shops she'd seen around the actual city while she was growing up.

Quinn tried to orient herself to the location when her hand brushed something hanging at her side.

It was the first time Quinn noticed she wasn't wearing the bodysuit from the testing room anymore. She wore blue jeans and a white tank top, with a black leather jacket topping the outfit.

She recognized the get-up immediately. It was the costume she'd chosen from a menu in a digital interface during her company orientation. Quinn remembered another selection she'd made that day, and her hand wrapped around the hilt of the broad-bladed Bowie knife hanging at her side. The bottom of the brown leather sheath had a strap that buckled mid-thigh to keep the blade from flopping when she moved.

Quinn smiled. This was her preferred avatar in the VR system, and she wished there was a mirror around somewhere so she could see how badass she looked. She wished Taylor could see her. Her friend was probably dressed in her own badass getup now.

A quick search of the rest of her clothes, including the pockets, turned up no other weapons or items of interest. Whatever she was supposed to be hunting, she was going to have to do it with the Bowie. She gripped the hilt tighter, pulling it free to examine it more closely. As she did, a brief burst of text hovered in front of her eyes for a few seconds in a transparent heads up display.

Bowie knife equipped.

As the text faded, something struck her from behind hard enough to almost knock her to her knees.

Staggering as she caught her balance, Quinn turned to see what it was.

She nearly screamed when she came face to face with a hairy, elongated snout filled with sharp fangs.

The wolf snarled at her but didn't attack. Instead, it turned and ran down the street. It loped along hunched over on two legs, occasionally reaching down with a clawed hand to help maintain balance as it ran. It had all happened so suddenly, she'd had no time to react before the creature ran on down the street.

Target acquired - Werewolf

The notification faded from her HUD, and Quinn realized the creature had already disappeared around the corner down the street to her right. She cursed and took off after it. She'd missed a perfect chance to take it out when it had run into her and she'd hesitated.

Pissed at herself for missing that opportunity, Quinn turned the corner and scanned the street.

Movement in the shadows on the sidewalk a hundred yards away drew her attention.

The werewolf had already run halfway down the next block.

Quinn pushed herself harder to pick up speed even as the wolf creature put more distance between them.

"Damn, I wish I was faster."

A message flashed in front of her.

Stamina may be spent to increase other abilities for a limited time.

Do you wish to draw upon your stamina score to increase your speed?

Quinn smiled and nodded. Her words spilled out between gasping breaths. "Yes, yes I do."

The HUD reappeared with a narrow green bar across the upper edge. As she watched, its length decreased by twenty-five percent, and it turned from dark green to a sort of pale lime hue as the value dropped. At the same time, there was a flare of searing cold against her breast bone.

Quinn's free hand went to her chest as her speed increased to an unnatural level and her fingertips brushed the familiar metal outline beneath her tank top. Somehow, her amulet was present here in the game. It was strange, though, and it felt like it was wrong somehow.

She didn't have the time to focus on the sense of wrongness. The crazy-fast speed boost she'd attained had given her just the amount of acceleration she'd needed to gain on her prey.

As she raced along, she laughed aloud, her voice carrying into the darkness of the empty street. Though Quinn had always been an athlete, this experience was both new and exhilarating. If only she'd been able to do this during the final state track meet of her high school career. She would've easily won instead of coming in fifth in the last race.

Quinn focused on the task at hand. She'd run fast enough that she'd caught up with her target. That speed boost had done the trick. She almost had him.

She reached out with her free hand to grab the werewolf's upper arm.

As her fingers brushed the fur, the werewolf's image flashed. For just a split second, Quinn raced inches behind a middle-aged balding man in khaki slacks and a white dress shirt.

The man glanced over his shoulder at her. The terror in his eyes made Quinn miss a step.

Was this a glitch in the system, or some kind of trick the creature used to fool her?

As she faltered and slowed, the creature switched back to its original form, snarling at her before running onward, pulling away once again as her speed boost ran out.

Quinn wondered what the heck she'd just seen. Something seemed off to her. Shaking her head, she ignored her internal voice and kept racing onward, pressing to gain on the beast once more.

As she ran after him, something new appeared in the upper right-hand corner of the HUD—a digital countdown now ticked off time. The words Mission Timer glowed over it in bright amber.

Only forty-seven seconds remained.

Great, she had to catch this thing and finish it off in a hurry if she was going to complete this first mission in time.

The VirSync team running the orientation classes had stressed several times that the company only intended to keep those whose abilities proved useful in helping them continue with successful tests.

She didn't know how many chances they'd give her to

succeed in a mission, but she definitely didn't want to fail her very first time out the gate.

Once again, Quinn called up the stamina drain feature she'd discovered and drew down another twenty-five percent of her stamina to boost her speed.

Once again, as she got closer to the werewolf, the image of the terrified balding man appeared for a split second before shifting back to the monster she'd been chasing.

This time, though, Quinn ignored it and didn't slow down. Instead, she pressed harder until she caught up with the werewolf again.

Maintaining her acceleration, Quinn waited until she was just a few feet behind the creature, then dove onto its back and stabbed down with the silver Bowie knife.

The creature rolled over as she hit it, raking at her stomach with its claws. A searing flash of very real pain hit her, but she pushed it aside. It wasn't like she was physically hurt, after all.

Her initial strike with her knife missed, so Quinn let her body weight and speed carry the werewolf to the ground.

It grunted as she landed atop it, then the beast kicked at her midsection, sending her to the pavement beside it.

Quinn sprang back to her feet, ready to defend herself against incoming attacks from the creature's claws and teeth.

She stopped, puzzled.

The strange, terrified man knelt on the sidewalk before her. "Please, I don't know why you're chasing me, but here, take my wallet and my watch. They are the only things of any value I have."

Quinn shook her head. "What the hell?"

"Please don't kill me. Please! I'm a father. I have children."

Quinn stood up, letting the hand wielding the Bowie to drop to her side.

"Where's the monster? Who are you?"

The man shook his head. "I don't know what monster you're talking about. I bumped into you back on that corner, and then you started chasing me with that knife."

Quinn cocked her head to one side, puzzled. "That wasn't what happened. You were a big hairy wolf-monster."

The man's eyes flashed understanding. His mouth opened, and he'd just started to say something when a black-clad figure dashed in from the left.

Quinn recognized the face; it was Fergus. Apparently, they were all playing in the same VR world instead of in independent scenarios.

The other hunter dove on top of the old man, pinning him to the sidewalk. Fergus's hand came up holding a shining silver tomahawk.

Quinn screamed. "No! He's—"

The hand hacked downward twice, and the man's pleas for mercy turned into a gurgling shriek.

She started to pull Fergus off of the old man, to try to render aid. As she did, the blinding pain and white light appeared once again. She stumbled and clutched her head.

Everything went black.

CHAPTER FOUR

Quinn lifted the goggles back up. It took a few seconds for her eyes to focus on the plain white ceiling tile above where she lay. She tried to think back to the training scenario. It had been shockingly real and graphic. It was also difficult to keep the details in her mind, almost as if it were a powerful dream or nightmare she'd had.

Sitting up, Quinn groaned as her hands went to her midsection. A flash of residual pain burned there where the werewolf had raked her with its claws. It still felt real.

When her hands met the smooth fabric of the Spandex bodysuit, Quinn tilted her head down to search her belly. She expected to find clawed rents in the fabric. Instead, she saw only the pristine skin-tight dark-gray fabric.

Quinn unbuckled the chinstrap and lifted the headpiece off, setting it in the cradle beside the exam couch. She wiped her forehead with the back of her hand. Her dark hair clung to the sweat there, plastered to the side of her face and scalp as if she'd been through a particularly heavy workout.

She swung her legs over the edge of the couch and stood. Quinn's legs wobbled like jelly, and she leaned back to steady herself against the exam table.

Across the room, the door opened.

Phillip stalked in, his finger raised and pointing in her direction. "You failed. Why didn't you kill your quarry?"

"I couldn't kill that nice old man. The monster I was chasing disappeared, then Fergus came and killed the old guy before I could do anything about it. It was like he didn't care if it was an old man or not."

Phillip stopped his advance and seemed startled for a second at her explanation, then his face darkened and he shook his head. "I don't know anything about any old man. You had a werewolf to track down and kill in that scenario. Fergus had already killed his target nearby. That was why he got a new target assigned—your target. It shouldn't have mattered, though, because you had plenty of time to do the job. That was your mission, and you failed."

Heat rose in Quinn's face and she turned red with anger as she reacted to his words. She didn't like it when anyone talked to her like that. It reminded her of too many abusive foster parents. She'd gotten out of those situations as fast as she could.

"I don't know what you expected me to do. I chased the werewolf, but then the VR system switched him into some helpless old man before I could kill the creature. I'm not some kind of heartless killing machine. If that's what you want, you can find someone else to do this job."

Phillip gestured to the door. "Go back to the locker

room and change. There'll be time to talk more about this during the debriefing."

He returned to the control room, leaving Quinn alone again.

Quinn's shoulders sagged. How did they expect her to play the game if she didn't understand the rules? The system had obviously glitched. Phillip's reaction when she'd explained what had happened inside the scenario told her that much. There was no way they expected her to kill ordinary people. What kind of program would train soldiers to do something so horrible?

Confused and defeated, Quinn stood and crossed the room, exiting through the door into the control room. Phillip and Velma stood talking beside the desk as she passed through the outer room. They stopped their conversation, watching her go by.

They didn't say anything to her.

Quinn didn't say anything, either. She stalked out and down the corridor to the locker room. In the back of her mind, she wondered if they'd fire her for failing the first mission. A part of her wouldn't be sorry if they did. The whole thing was weird.

Another part of her, though, got obstinate, the more she thought about what had happened. She wasn't going to let their glitchy system stop her from being successful, and she'd tell them as much when the time came for debriefing.

CHAPTER FIVE

Laughter echoed through the locker room as Quinn entered. The other candidates smiled and chattered with each other about their experiences in the testing system.

Taylor ran over and grabbed Quinn's arm. "Wasn't it totally awesome? I've never done anything so thrilling in my life. It felt like the whole thing was real, and, damn, when that thing's blood splattered my face, I thought it was going to start burning through my skin or something. What kind of demons do you think they were?"

"You had a demon?"

Taylor nodded. "It had scales all over its body and horns growing from its forehead, so I guess that's what it was. Why, what did you run into?"

Quinn shook her head. "I don't know. At first, mine was some sort of werewolf or something. Maybe they're all demons of one sort or another."

"Really, a werewolf? That's awesome, too. I wonder

how many different kinds of creatures there were? I need to ask the others."

Taylor glanced at the four other women changing out of their bodysuits and back into their normal street clothes.

All Quinn could do was let out a short, forced chuckle. She didn't understand why she'd had such a different experience. Everyone else seemed to have avoided whatever glitch affected her.

Taylor spun back to Quinn instead of going over to talk to the other candidates. "Oh, did you hear? One of the other girls heard their system managers talking as she left the room. Somebody screwed up and gave another candidate a chance at a second kill, so one of the boys was able to score two kills in one session. I wouldn't want to be the one who failed their first mission. Remember when they told us that could get us fired?"

Quinn grimaced. It wasn't going to take people long to figure out it was her. Fergus knew who she was, even if no one else let them know it was her. He'd seemed nice enough in the parking lot, but that didn't mean he wouldn't gloat about taking her kill.

Quinn said, "Yeah, well, maybe whatever happened was the result of some sort of glitch in the system. It was probably nobody's fault."

"Wait a minute. You make it sound like you were the one who missed the target. You just said you had a werewolf in your scenario. You got the kill, didn't you?"

Quinn glanced at the others to make sure they weren't listening to the two of them, then turned back to Taylor. "I'd rather not broadcast it for everyone to hear, Taylor.

Hopefully, they don't make a big deal out of it when we go to the debriefing. Like I said, I think it was a glitch in the system."

Taylor leaned in and whispered, "Quinn, what happened? Of all people here, I never expected you to have a problem with anything like this. You love showing off your martial arts skills, and you're so competitive all the time. I would've thought you would have gotten the kill before anyone else did."

Quinn shook her head. She didn't know how to explain the queasy feeling she had inside or the uncertainty about what else she'd seen inside the game.

Thankfully, when Quinn didn't answer, Taylor let it drop.

Quinn was about to ask her friend about her experience inside the simulator when a woman in a dark skirt and blazer came in.

"Stop the jabbering, ladies. Everyone is expected in the trainees' auditorium for a debriefing session in five minutes. We have some interesting things to discuss with you regarding this evening's session, including a special award to one of the candidates for a unique achievement. Hurry up and get changed. Everyone is expected to be there and seated before our CEO, Mr. Hickman, arrives to make the presentation."

The woman spun and left, and Quinn turned back to her locker. She peeled off the bodysuit and tossed it into a laundry bin in the center of the room, then she started to get dressed.

She had a good idea of who was getting an award and why. If it was Fergus, it was equally likely they'd point out who had allowed him the opportunity to bag the second kill. This whole evening was starting to totally suck.

Quinn wondered if she could sneak out and avoid the debriefing altogether. She didn't think it would bode well for her if she wasn't there to be called out for her failure in the testing session. The whole thing left her grinding her teeth in anger and frustration.

Caught up in the midst of pondering her situation, Quinn looked up and realized she was the last one in the locker room. She grabbed her bag and headed out to catch up with Taylor and the others. The woman who'd made the announcement stood in the hall outside and glared at her when she walked through the locker room door.

Quinn returned the glare and shifted to the other side of the hall to walk around her.

The woman grabbed at Quinn's arm when she tried to pass by. "Ms. Faust, please take a seat in the back row, center. There'll be a piece of tape with your name on the seatback."

Quinn had no idea what to say in response, so she simply nodded and picked up her pace to follow the others she saw farther down the hallway. She caught up as they reached the door that led into a small auditorium that looked like it could seat about fifty people. Everyone moved down front and grabbed seats in the first few rows. There were about a dozen candidates, male and female.

As instructed by the woman outside the locker room, Quinn looked for a seat marked with her name. She spotted it and slid into the third row. She sat down and noticed Taylor seated right in front of her. Her friend sat with Fergus on her left. She had an open seat to her right.

"Quinn, I saved you a seat."

"I'm supposed to sit here. See, there's my name." Quinn pointed to the tape with her name.

Taylor mouthed the word, "Oh," and turned around as the persistent murmur of young voices in the room trailed off.

A tall, dark-haired man wearing black slacks and a white dress shirt open at the collar walked onto the stage and stood behind the wooden podium set off to one side.

He stared out at them and waited for a few seconds until the silence in the room was complete before he began speaking. "My name is Myles Hickman, and I'm the CEO of VirSync. I dropped by this debriefing to tell you how excited we are to have such a group of talented young people like you helping us develop the future of VR training technology. We've come a long way in our testing and research to get here, but it all comes down to this program now to prove it works. If you can demonstrate the effectiveness of it as a testing and training system with real-world applications, this will be, if you'll excuse the pun, a game-changer."

He paused and waited for the chuckles that popped up around the room at his attempt at humor.

Quinn would've groaned and smiled if she hadn't feared what had to be coming next. Her expectation wasn't off the mark.

Myles smiled at the assembled candidates and their reaction to his bad joke as he continued, "There are some things to commend in today's first session, and there are also a few things that will need special attention to make sure they don't happen again. In that line of thought, I'd like to bring one of our candidates to the stage. Fergus Bishop is one of our exceedingly talented testers from today. He made an unprecedented two kills in one session."

Myles shaded his eyes to look out through the bright lights to see where Fergus was.

Fergus stood up, raising his arms over his head and clasping his hands like a champion boxer receiving acclaim in the ring.

Applause filled the small auditorium.

He made his way past the other people in his row to the aisle and bounded up onto the stage.

Myles greeted Fergus with a firm handshake and a pat on the back. They exchanged a few words before parting, with Fergus standing next to Myles and facing the others with a huge smile on his face.

The CEO turned back to the rest of them. "This is exactly the kind of astute and hard-driving effort we want to see from all of you. We need you to push our system to the limit and beyond. The only way to ensure you do that is to reinforce that you're in competition with each other. We are timing you to see who can complete their missions the fastest and using the most direct methods. People like Fergus here will be rewarded. People like the candidate who couldn't kill their primary target, giving him the opportunity to locate and kill it, will be recognized as well for their failure. That person deserves their punishment."

Quinn stiffened in her seat at his final statement. She didn't like the way he said that. What workplace talked to its employees that way? Punishment was a strange choice of words. Quinn didn't have a lot of work experience to draw on, though, so she didn't know for sure.

Myles leaned into the microphone again while he stared out through the lights at the assembled candidates. "Will Quinn Faust please stand? You do not need to come up on the stage. This space is reserved for champions and the best among you."

Quinn glanced around the room. A few of the people from her orientation group knew her by name. They all turned in her direction. Taylor offered the only sympathetic face.

Quinn stood as requested, her hands at her sides, fists clenched in anger. She hated being singled out this way. She didn't understand how it was her fault that something went wrong with their system. She'd had nothing to do it.

Quinn started to sit when he started talking again, thinking he was finished with her.

No such luck.

"No, don't sit down, Miss Faust. It's important for people to understand that we are very serious about success here at the VirSync. We do not work on anything that is not the best it can be. Since this is your first day in the testing program, we will make the punishment for your failure the embarrassment you're feeling while you stand here in front of the other candidates. We want everyone to know they'll be singled out for this particular dishonor if they fail."

Quinn's face burned. She wished she could turn away or sit back down again. She knew better than that, though. Myles Hickman had meant it when he told her to remain standing, and she still wanted to make this job work out, if only to prove she was capable of succeeding the next time out.

JAMIE DAVIS

"I want all of you to take a hard look at Miss Faust standing there. She screwed up and hesitated. She could've made the kill, but she didn't follow through at the last critical instant. We want this system to bring out the best in the people we train in it. That means we can't show mercy. We must strive for complete victory at all times. When you're assigned a target in the game, you're expected to complete your mission as fast as possible. I hope I do not have to make an example of anyone else in the future like this. I think you will all agree it will not be a pleasant experience should it happen."

Myles waved his hand in Quinn's direction. "Sit down." His dismissive gesture as he turned back to Fergus and pointed at him as he began clapping for the day's recognized winner.

Fergus stood on stage, grinning like an idiot and soaking up the recognition before the group. He kept his hands at his sides and his shoulders back as if he were standing at attention in some sort of military unit.

Myles continued when the applause subsided again. "Instead of being like Miss Faust, I recommend you emulate Mr. Bishop here. Mr. Bishop, you may return to your seat."

Myles waited by the podium as Fergus jumped down from the edge of the stage and returned to his seat. As he passed the other candidates, he exchanged high-fives and grins with several of them. He slid into his seat next to Taylor, pausing and shooting Quinn a broad, toothy grin before settling in beside her best friend and throwing his arm around her shoulders.

Taylor shrugged off the arm, shifting away from Fergus.

He just laughed and turned his attention to the girl seated on his other side.

That girl, a perky blond named Cindy, squealed with delight and leaned into Fergus' one-armed hug.

From the stage, Myles laughed at the display of affection given to Fergus by the other candidates. "To the victor go the spoils. It seems like you've already started to get your reward, Mr. Bishop."

Laughter spread through the other candidates as they turned around to look at Fergus and Cindy.

Quinn groaned. This whole thing was the worst.

Taylor reached back and gave her friend's hand a squeeze.

Quinn forced a smile. Taylor was always there for her when she needed it.

Myles went back to talking about what was expected of them, and Quinn's mind drifted for a few seconds. A sort of daze passed over her as he droned on in the background. It almost sounded like he'd shifted to speaking in a different language.

Quinn shook her head a few seconds later and forced herself to focus on what the CEO was saying from the stage. He seemed to be wrapping up his speech. She glanced at her phone to check the time, hoping they wouldn't be here too much longer.

Her eyes widened. The late hour surprised Quinn. She had no idea they'd been here that long. It was already past one in the morning. What could Myles Hickman have talked about for hours like that?

That couldn't be right. Where had all the time gone?

By Quinn's estimate, it should only have been about

two hours since she'd arrived at VirSync, not going on seven.

Her time in the VR world had amounted to no more than four or five minutes, although, now that she tried to remember what had happened, she couldn't. All she could remember was that she'd failed to kill her target and Fergus had taken it from her. She couldn't remember any specifics. She felt like there was something important she was missing. The fact that the details of what she had done in the system test had slipped from her memory bugged her.

Quinn checked the time again. It didn't make sense.

She went over the night's activities again. The rest of her time here in the VirSync building should've been no more than two, maybe three hours, between the prep and getting changed in the locker room. There were three or four hours she couldn't account for.

Quinn glanced around while she tried to understand where the missing time had gone. Everyone had their eyes glued to the stage and the CEO's continuing speech on excellence.

They couldn't have been sitting here listening to the speech for that long. The only thing that accounted for the lost time was that something else had happened during the perceived five minutes inside the testing system. It bothered Quinn to think she'd been lying there in the testing room that whole time. It didn't make sense.

Myles said a few more words of encouragement before dismissing the group.

As Quinn left the room, she found herself preoccupied with the problem of the missing time. She wanted to ask

Taylor about it to see if she remembered her experience in the test scenario.

Several of the candidates sneered at her as she walked out, and she ignored them.

Fergus came over with Cindy beside him. "Quinn, I can't believe you let that kill get away from you. You were standing right there with your blade in hand, ready to go. All you had to do was finish the thing off."

"It wasn't as simple as that," Quinn argued. She struggled to remember the details of what happened in there but couldn't. She simply replied, "I don't know what you saw in there, but my system was all glitched up."

"Well, I hope they fix that problem for your sake. If you're gonna freeze up like that every time we go into the system, I'm going to have stay close to you. I don't want to miss a second double-kill day."

Cindy smiled as she ran her hand up Fergus's muscular arm.

Quinn rolled her eyes. She looked for Taylor and saw her talking to a few of the other candidates nearby.

Fergus turned away from Quinn and started chatting with two other candidates.

Quinn went over to join Taylor, where she stood with the others.

"Quinn, I'm so sorry about what happened in there. I hope they fix it for you. I was talking with Claire and Gary here about what we saw of the program they were using in the control room to run the VR system. They're both coders."

Quinn nodded a greeting. "Hey, I'm tired, and I want to get out of here. You ready to head home?"

"Claire mentioned something about going out for something to eat at an all-night diner she knows about nearby. I thought I'd tag along to talk some more about the amazing computer systems they have here. Do you want to come?"

"Uh, no, that's all right. I'm going to head home. I've got a major migraine starting, probably caused by my broken VR setup."

"You don't mind if I go with them, do you?"

Claire nodded. "Don't worry, we'll make sure she gets home in one piece."

Quinn chuckled at the situation. One sure way to lure Taylor away from a good night's sleep was to offer her an opportunity to talk about computers, hacking, and everything in between.

Quinn smiled and said, "Sure, whatever. Just remember we have to be back at work tomorrow evening. I know how you get when people start talking circuit boards and bits and bytes."

"I won't be too late, I'm sure," Taylor said, laughing as she glanced at Claire and Gary. "Don't wait up, though."

Quinn didn't say anything. Taylor could take care of herself. She waved at them and headed back down the hallway toward the lobby and parking lot.

She was glad Taylor had found like-minded friends in the group. For Quinn, this day sucked more with each passing minute. She just wanted to get home.

Her earlier doubts about the job had turned into serious questions about what had happened to her tonight. She needed to get out of here and clear her mind.

CHAPTER SIX

Quinn left the building and headed across the dark parking lot toward her Jeep. As she walked, she wondered why her mind was in such a fog when she thought about the questions surrounding the lost hours inside the testing room. She couldn't remember more than a few details of what had happened when she'd failed to kill her target. It was like she was forgetting something important. The harder she tried to think of it, the more she felt like it was slipping out of her grasp.

She got to where her Jeep sat under a lamppost. Quinn stood in the pool of light from the overhead lamp and shook her head, trying to clear the cobwebs.

The strange feeling had to be related to the VR training system in some way. The missing hours from the earlier part of the evening weren't any clearer than the missing memories she tried to bring back.

She'd have to remember to say something when she came back to work the next evening. Phillip and Velma should be told. If there was some sort of problem with the system they were using, the company should know about it, even if it seemed to have no effect on the other candidates.

Quinn unlocked the door and climbed into the Jeep. Starting it, she let the engine warm up as she idly flipped through the notifications on her phone. A news alert came up in one of them, with a small photo next to it.

She froze.

The news headline swam in and out of focus because her eyes stayed glued to the face of the man in the photo. She tapped it to launch the article in a browser.

The face appeared again, larger this time, filling the screen. It was so familiar that it sent chills down her spine and raised goosebumps on her arms.

It was the man from the training simulation. The one she couldn't kill.

Why had she been trying to kill him, anyway?

The fog drifted back over her memories as if something was trying to force her to think about something else. Quinn had to force herself to stay focused on the article. She stared at the picture, willing herself to remember.

The guy in the photo wore glasses, and it looked as if it had been pulled from a driver's license or something like that. In the picture, he was in front of an American flag and a plain white background.

Quinn scrolled down, bringing up the article to learn more about why his face had shown up in her news feed.

The article was a breaking news story about the death of an important politician from the city of Baltimore. He'd recently been found brutally murdered on a city street near his home.

She kept reading the article. As she did, the fog lifted from her mind, clearing the way for the full collection of the night's memories to flood back into her. They came on like crashing waves as she read an eyewitness account from a person who'd been there when the body was discovered on the sidewalk.

"One bystander, who declined to be identified to this reporter, said, 'I couldn't believe it. I've never seen anything so gross in my life. It was like he'd been hacked to bits with a hatchet or something.'"

Quinn froze. The description brought to her mind a visual of Fergus using his weapon of choice, a tomahawk, on her target in the game. That target, whether it was a monstrous werewolf or an old man, was one she hadn't been able to bring herself to kill in cold blood.

She scrolled up to the top of the article and the photograph of the politician. Quinn started trembling as she realized that somehow, the man she'd seen in the testing system had been a real person. Not only that, but he'd been murdered on the same night she'd hunted him through virtual city streets in a VR game that looked a lot like downtown Baltimore.

How could that be?

Quinn's mind swam through possible explanations. Maybe there was an internet mixup during the VR session, and the system had grabbed this guy's image from the web, where it was plastered all over the news.

It could be as simple as that, couldn't it?

Quinn tried to calm her breathing. She'd been hyper-ventilating. She didn't know what to think about this. There was no explanation for how the man in the murder story had ended up in her VR training session.

She also couldn't explain how the man had died in a very similar manner to what she'd remembered from the system.

Was it a coincidence? Could coincidence explain why things matched so exactly?

Quinn made up her mind. She had to know more. She re-read the top portion of the article and quickly found out what she wanted. Quinn put the Jeep in drive and pulled out of the parking space, heading for the parking lot's exit.

As she drove through the gate and onto the road, Quinn feared what she might find when she got into the city. That fear didn't deter her, though. She had to know the answer, no matter what. There'd be no sleep or rest for her until she got an answer.

Once she'd reached the Beltway, Quinn headed for the exit that would take her into the east Baltimore neighbor-hood she'd seen mentioned in the article. It wouldn't take her too long. There wouldn't be much traffic at this time of night.

Quinn arrived downtown a half-hour later. She drove around a little, trying to get her bearings. She looked for anything that seemed familiar and might trigger a memory of something impossible.

She found it.

Pulling over, Quinn stopped the Jeep and sat there on

the neighborhood street, staring at the corner grocery store.

After sliding the gear shift into Park, Quinn climbed out and stood on the sidewalk, staring around at the familiar two- and three-story row homes and shops exactly like the ones she'd seen earlier in the evening while she was inside the VirSync testing and training system.

Quinn glanced over her shoulder, half-expecting to be shoved from behind by a running werewolf trying to get past her. Of course, there was no one else there. An occasional car drove by a cross street in the distance, but this street sat empty for now.

She shook her head. "No, no, this can't be real. Get hold of yourself, Quinn."

Not sure what to do other than retrace her virtual steps from earlier, Quinn crossed the street and proceeded to the corner by the store. She stopped and peered around the side at a cluster of police vehicles and news vans, and the yellow crime scene tape strung across from one sidewalk to the other.

Like a moth drawn to a hot light bulb, Quinn started down the street until she reached the crime scene tape. Aside from the police and news vehicles, it all looked just like what she'd seen in the VR system. Dark, dried blood stained the cement sidewalk where the body had lain.

Quinn noticed a police officer walking in her direction, and she backed away from the line of caution tape. She gave the officer a half-wave, shoved her hands in her jeans pocket, and started back toward the corner. As she turned to leave, she jostled a tall man in a shabby dark overcoat who was standing just behind her.

Startled that she hadn't spotted him before, she looked into his face. She couldn't see much because he had his baseball cap pulled down over his eyes.

It was odd that he was wearing an overcoat in such warm weather, but she'd seen a lot of weird stuff while she'd lived on the streets when she was younger. A lot of the homeless wore everything they owned to keep from losing anything.

Quinn held up her hands and backed up a step. Assuming he *was* homeless, she said, "Sorry, I don't have any cash on me."

The man didn't say anything, just stepped to one side so she could walk past and nodded.

Quinn took the opportunity to make her exit. She turned to look back after taking a few steps to make sure he wasn't following her.

He wasn't following her. He wasn't *there*.

Quinn stopped and looked around. There was no way he could have gotten out of her line of sight that quickly, yet there was no sign of him anywhere.

For a moment, Quinn considered going back to ask the police officer watching her from behind the police tape where the guy had gone. Then she decided she'd had too many strange things happen tonight already. If she talked to the officer, he might wonder what she was doing up and about at this time of night. She didn't need to try to explain why she'd come to this crime scene in the middle of the night.

Quinn backed up a few steps, still scanning the area for the guy. Then she turned and headed at a fast walk back up the street toward her Jeep.

She had to figure out what was happening. A crazy, horrible idea explained it all, but Quinn knew it had to be wrong.

No, not just wrong...

It was impossible, wasn't it?

Her mind whirled, searching for a possible explanation as she stopped at the all-night grocery and went inside to grab a soda. Maybe that would help wake her up so she could think clearly.

CHAPTER SEVEN

Quinn unscrewed the cap on the soda as she left the grocery store and drained half the bottle to try to clear the foul taste of bile from her mouth. She'd been queasy and on the edge of vomiting ever since she'd seen where the man had died.

Occupied by a swirling vortex of thoughts about what had happened to her and the murder victim earlier that evening, Quinn crossed the street and approached her Jeep. A flash of cold beneath her t-shirt went almost unnoticed. Without conscious thought, Quinn reached into her collar and lifted the chain so the pendant rested on top of the fabric rather than against her skin.

She pulled open the driver's door and climbed into the Jeep, setting the bottled soda in the cupholder. She started the engine and pulled away from the curb, doing a U-turn to head back up the street toward the highway.

It was late, and despite her earlier desire to think things through, all she wanted now was to get some sleep. Maybe if she sorted things out overnight in her dreams, they would look better. She'd see if her subconscious mind had an answer to all the questions going through her head.

Quinn hadn't gone more than three blocks back up the street when something cold and sharp pressed against her neck, startling her to the point she swerved.

A man's voice whispered in Quinn's ear from behind, "Don't slow down, keep driving. I'll tell you where to go."

Oh, my God, she had known it was a bad idea to drive into the city this late at night alone. She usually had more street smarts than that. Now someone had snuck into her Jeep and was trying to...well, she didn't know what.

Quinn sucked in a sharp breath as she regained control of the vehicle and looked into the rearview mirror. She recognized the ball cap, although the face was still hidden by the visor's shadow. It was the vagrant from the crime scene.

Clearing her throat, Quinn said, "Look, I don't have a lot of money. I don't know what you want from me, but I'm sure we can come to an understanding. I'll give you what I have."

"I won't hurt you as long as I get the answers to the questions I have. Now shut up and drive."

Quinn didn't know what answers he wanted from her —and it was a small relief if he was telling the truth about what he wanted—but he was still holding a knife to her throat.

She kept going up the street, searching her mind for some way to disable her attacker. Her mind rolled through her options as she drove through the dark residential streets. It was likely he'd make her drive to some secluded area where he could ask his questions or worse. She couldn't let that happen.

As the Jeep approached the highway, she shifted toward the on-ramp. The deep, gravelly voice hissed in her ear, "No! Stay off the highway. Keep going straight, then take a left at that traffic light up ahead."

"Tell me where you're taking me. I'm not gonna let you drive me somewhere you can just kill me and dump my body."

The man chuckled. "You've got guts, I'll give you that. You're not too smart, though. I'm the one with a knife to your throat, and you're trying to make demands of me?"

"If all you want is information, just ask me your questions while we drive, and then I'll let you out."

"Not here. Take a left at the light and keep driving. There's a city park with a public lot up ahead. Park there, where we can have some privacy."

Quinn grimaced. This was exactly what she'd feared.

As she turned left and headed down the street, she saw the parking lot ahead, next to a baseball diamond. The area was open and well-lit, but a stand of trees nearby would be a great place to hide her body if that's what he wanted to do. At this hour, it was unlikely anyone was paying any attention to the parking lot.

"Pull into the entrance and drive to the back corner. No one will bother us there."

Quinn did as the man said, as she started to form a plan to get away from him. She drove up the slight incline into the lot, letting her left hand drop down beside her seat and rest there while she steered with her right hand.

When she pulled into the parking space, Quinn

stomped on the brake so hard the Jeep jolted to a sudden stop. At the same time, she pulled up on the seat handle with her left hand. As they both lurched forward and then back with the sudden stop, she pushed back hard with both legs, reclining her seat against the attacker in back.

When he grunted in surprise, she lifted her left leg and planted a foot against the dashboard, then pressed backward with all her might, slamming the seat back into the man and pinning him to the back seat.

He immediately began to twist, trying to get out from under the front seat. Quinn wrestled with him for control of the blade, successfully pulling it away from her throat before it could cause more damage.

A warm trickle of blood flowed down her neck to drip onto the headrest, but it didn't feel like the wound was serious. The knife hadn't done much damage during their gyrations.

Quinn renewed her struggle to control the weapon. Even with two hands, though, she was hard-pressed to hold the knife at bay. The corded muscle of his forearm might as well have been an iron bar. It resisted her efforts to pull the blade more than an inch from her neck.

Luckily, she'd managed to trap his other arm behind the seat so he couldn't bring it to bear, at least not yet.

The problem was, they were in a stalemate.

Quinn wanted to escape the vehicle but couldn't let go to try to open her door or unbuckle her seatbelt so she could slip away. He was too strong. The instant she let go, he'd plunge the knife home and end her.

As she struggled to gain more leverage, the man wriggled behind her.

Quinn lifted her right leg up to push against the dash along with her left. Using both legs, she pressed back harder. If she could just hold him off a little longer, she might be able to come up with a plan to disarm him and get away.

Realizing it was a desperate moment calling for desperate action, Quinn tilted her head forward. She opened her mouth and bit down as hard as she could on the hand holding the knife.

The coppery taste of blood washed across her tongue as her teeth broke the skin.

The man howled in pain but didn't let go of the knife. Quinn bit down harder, grinding her teeth in as he strained, trying to break free of her hands and teeth.

She continued to press down with her teeth, tearing the skin and muscle of his hand, and finally, the knife fell away.

The blade dropped to the floor beside the seat, out of sight and reach.

Quinn let go of his wrist with her left hand and reached out, trying to open the door. The instant she let go, though, the man overpowered her. He slammed his forearm against her head and yanked back, pulling his arm free.

Quinn was stretching her left arm to reach the door handle when he punched the side of her face.

She glimpsed it coming out of the corner of her eye and twisted to the side at the last second, so the descending fist landed only a glancing blow.

The impact still struck with enough force to cause Quinn to see stars. She gasped in pain as he crashed his fist into her face and head again and again.

Twisting around in the seat to get away from his blows,

she groped to the side, trying to reach the door's handle. This time she succeeded and managed to pop the door.

Swinging her legs around and leaning forward, Quinn reached for the doorframe to haul herself out of the Jeep. A bloody hand clamped down on her shoulder, holding her back, followed by another.

With two hands clamped on her shoulders, the man pulled her backward and sideways into the car so that her back slammed painfully against the center console. He'd finally managed to free himself from the front seat.

Now the attacker leaned over her while she flailed at him, kicking out with her feet in a futile effort to gain purchase door frame.

The man pressed down on her chest with his bloodied right hand and raised his fist, ready to slam it into her face again.

Then he stopped.

Quinn winced, expecting the blow to land any second.

Instead of striking her, though, the eyes peering out from beneath the baseball cap's visor stared down at her.

The raised fist beside his head opened, and his index finger extended, pointing downward.

"Where did you get that."

"Where did I get what?"

Quinn glanced down at her chest and realized he was pointing at her pendant.

"Look, it's just a silver pendant, but if you want it, take it and get out of here."

"I don't want it. I want to know how you got it."

"I got it from my parents, okay? Just take it and go."

"Who are your parents? Where did they get it?"

"Look, I'm not here to tell you my life story."

The man growled at her. "Where. Did. You. Get. It?"

"It was left with me as a baby. I've been told it was the only thing I had when they found me. Look, just take the pendant, take my wallet, take my Jeep. Just leave me be."

The man leaned forward, giving her the first good luck at his face. The light shining in from the parking lot lights illuminated his features.

The skin on his face had the look of worn leather. It was tanned and aged and had fine wrinkles, especially around the eyes and at the corners of his mouth. Several days' worth of stubble covered his jaw, and he had a narrow white scar across the bridge of his nose and down his right cheek.

"If you answer my questions, I won't hurt you. I told you earlier, I just want answers. I don't want your money. I don't want your Jeep. I don't want you. I just want answers, now even more than before."

"Fine. Let go of me, and I'll give you your answers."

The man grinned and shook his head. "I'm not stupid, you know. I'm not letting go of you. You'll just run away and make me chase you."

Several long seconds of silence passed between them.

Quinn realized they'd reached an impasse. He couldn't let go, and she couldn't get away. At least he'd stopped punching her.

She sighed, giving in for now. "What do you want to know?"

"I want to know what you were doing back there."

"Back where? You mean, back on the street where that man was killed?" Quinn wondered what the hell this guy had to do with that. He couldn't be a cop. She could spot a cop from a mile away. Maybe he was some kind of private investigator. "I was just out for a drive and saw the police lights. I was only curious."

The man's nostrils flared and he shook his head again. "I can tell when you lie to me. Tell me the truth. There was something about you. I sensed it when you bumped into me. I don't know how, but you had something to do with what happened there. You know who killed that man."

"Look, if you think I killed him, I didn't. I just saw the thing on the news and wanted to come down to see where it happened. That's all, I swear."

The man tilted his head to the side and drew a deep breath through his nose. He smiled. "You're lying. I can smell it."

Quinn started to laugh, then got the sense from the look in his eyes he wasn't kidding. He flared his nostrils again as if trying to discern even more about her. Of course, that was ridiculous.

He seemed to believe it, though. He'd also been correct so far.

"I was curious about how he died. That's all. Now let me go."

"If you keep telling the same lie, we'll be here all night. Since you won't answer that, maybe you'll explain to me again where you got the amulet."

"What? Why are you obsessed with my pendant? I told you, when I was abandoned as a baby, it was the only thing with me other than a blanket, a note, and the clothes I was wearing. I was left at a fire station here in the city. I never knew who my parents were. All they left was this pendant and a note that said, 'Her name is Quinn.'"

"When was this?"

"Eighteen years ago, why?"

He lifted his gaze and got a distant look in his eyes, as if he stared out the windshield at something far away. Quinn craned her neck, trying to see what he was looking at.

Realizing he was distracted by something, she tensed, preparing to pull away.

His grip tightened before she could move a muscle.

"Don't. Let me think. None of this makes any sense."

"None of what makes any sense? You're the one speaking in riddles."

The man looked down at her. "If I let you up, do you promise not to run away? I'm not here to hurt you, but I need answers. I know you're involved somehow with what happened back there. I have your license number and enough of a description that if I gave it to the police, they'd surely track you down. Something tells me you don't want that kind of trouble."

Quinn thought about that. She didn't have much love for the police. They would take one look at her juvenile record as a runaway, a shoplifter, and her other, similar crimes and make assumptions about her involvement in the man's death. She wasn't even sure there wasn't any physical evidence tied to her at the scene. Quinn didn't want to take the chance.

She accepted now that she'd been there, somehow. She

still didn't understand how she'd gone from being inside a virtual reality simulation fifteen miles away, well outside the city, to being in the middle of a downtown neighborhood.

Quinn considered the matter of the missing time she couldn't account for. Could they have somehow transported her downtown, used some sort of hypnotism or drugs to make her forget the trip, and then return back to the test center in time for her and the others to all wake up?

It seemed far-fetched.

Quinn didn't want to take the chance that it had all been real, though. The police wouldn't take long to figure it out either if this random homeless guy had seen it.

Quinn relaxed her tense body. "Okay, I won't run as long as you don't try to hurt me anymore."

The man nodded and slowly released his grip on her shoulders. He pointed to the passenger seat beside her. "Slide over there. I'll climb into the driver's seat. Then we'll talk."

Quinn pushed herself up and over the center console, swinging her legs around until she sat in the passenger seat, facing front. She put her hands on her knees, the fingertips of her right hand inches from the door's handle. She was ready to pop it open the instant he made another move in her direction.

She watched his every move as he slid behind the steering wheel. He raised the seatback until it was in position, then pulled the driver's door closed.

"Let's start with introductions. You said your name is Quinn?"

She nodded. "And you?"

"My name is Clark, and until now, I thought I was the last survivor of the local hunter clans."

CHAPTER EIGHT

Quinn waited after his pronouncement, expecting him to say more in explanation. The whole thing was cryptic, to say the least.

Clark stared at Quinn, his eyes boring into hers as if mining for unspoken answers in response to what he said.

Quinn glared back at him. "Is that supposed to mean something to me?"

Clark gestured at Quinn's pendant. "It should. You're wearing a hunter's amulet."

Clark reached under his collar and fished out a silver chain only a little thicker than hers. At the end of the chain dangled an amulet identical to hers, and he turned it to show her both sides.

Quinn looked at him after staring at his silver pendant for what seemed like forever. Time seemed to stop as she met his tired, dark eyes. "How? How are they the same?"

"I don't know. I thought they were all destroyed during the purges that started twenty years ago. It could be a knockoff, but I don't think so. Let me ask you a question.

Has the amulet ever done anything strange or felt odd any time when you were touching it?"

Quinn didn't answer. What had once been a childhood fantasy about a magic charm left to her by her parents was really a secret tool she'd used to keep herself out of trouble.

When she didn't answer right away, Clark snorted a laugh. "Your silence is all the answer I need. Now I know it's real."

Irritation bubbled up inside Quinn. "How do you know? I didn't say anything."

Clark lifted his amulet to dangle from his fingertip. "This amulet and others like it are infused with powerful protections and charms. They shield me from spells or attacks that might influence my mind or injure me in some way. It's not foolproof, but it gives me an edge against surprise attacks, both magical and mundane. It can do other things, but only for those trained in its use."

He nodded at Quinn's pendant. "Even for an untrained person or child, the protections would operate at some level. The magic is quite intuitive."

Quinn shook her head. "Magic? You expect me to believe magic is real, and you have some sort of mystical powers.?"

"You don't believe me?"

"Why should I?"

"Because you reek of it, and powerful magic at that. You've had at least one major spell cast on you in the last twenty-four hours, if not more. I can sense that much. Then there's your association with the attack on the coun-cilman. I was shadowing him, offering what protection I could when I was available. He slipped away from me today, as he liked to do sometimes. By the time I caught up with him earlier this evening, he'd already been attacked and killed. Bystanders said they saw nothing. A few claimed to have seen shadowy, ghostlike figures clustered around the victim."

Clark growled, "Whoever they were, the attackers disappeared without a trace. I found trails leading away in two directions, but they ended a few steps away from where he was killed. There was no evidence left at the scene. I tasted the residual magic that remained, though. It had the same taint as the spell that's been cast on you."

Quinn shook her head and laughed. None of this made sense. A few days before, she would have assumed Clark was an insane homeless person.

After the events of the night, she wasn't so sure.

Quinn didn't know what was real anymore. Her experience today with the VR system at VirSync, the strangely related death of the city councilman, and now these crazy claims by Clark, a man who thought he could smell magic on her, shook her understanding of reality to its core.

Quinn reached for the door handle. "This is all too much. There's no such thing as magic. I need to get out of here."

As she did, Clark waved two fingers of one hand in a circular movement, and the door locks engaged. She tried to unlock the door, but it wouldn't open for her, no matter what she did.

Quinn spun to face Clark. "How'd you do that?"

He smiled. "Magic, what else? You may try to deny its existence. Most people do, but that's because they don't know about the hidden battle going on out of sight all around them. A fight happening in the sort of dark shadows most people avoid."

Clark pointed at her amulet. "You know about magic. Your amulet has protected you, even though you don't know how to use its full abilities. Has someone ever attacked you from behind or tried to sneak up on you? The amulet warned you just before they were able to launch their surprise or attack, am I right?"

Quinn had always called it her magic, but she hadn't really believed it. Her little-girl self had called them her cold warnings. She'd always chalked it up to her imagination and wishful thinking. What kid didn't want to believe they had magical powers of some kind?

She'd always sort of known, hadn't she?

She'd used the magic as she grew older, even though she pretended it was a childish fantasy. Whether it was to avoid contact in a fast-paced lacrosse game, or even when a friend tried to sneak up and surprise her, Quinn always knew when to step to the side or shift direction.

Even given her understanding of it now from Clark, it was a lot to confront when the reality of magic smacked her in the face like this.

Quinn leaned back in her seat and settled herself. She glanced at the locked door and then at Clark. Her pendant —no, he'd called it her "amulet"—wasn't warning her anymore, like it had tried to when she'd ignored it getting into the Jeep earlier. She figured she was safe for now.

Clark hadn't made a move to hurt her, at least not since his initial attack. His blade was still on the floor beside the driver's seat, unless he had some way to teleport it back to himself.

Of course, he wouldn't let her out of the car, either.

Quinn decided she was entitled to answers of her own. "All right, I'll bite. What do you mean by a hidden fight in the shadows?"

"Our world sits at a nexus, a sort of gateway between the planes of light and the planes of darkness. We don't know why this is so, only that it has been that way for as long as the hunter histories have been kept."

Quinn remained silent and waited for more explanation.

Clark continued, "There are some who believe our world was created for that purpose, to serve as a meeting ground between the two opposing forces of the universe. That necessary neutral ground keeps the universe from devolving into chaos as the two sides fight a war where no one wins."

"Instead of using it to just meet, they use our world, our Earth, and those who inhabit it, to meet, negotiate, and seek opportunities for advantage over the other. It might have saved the universe, but it has made our world a battleground."

"Millennia ago, hunter clans rose up to defend mankind against incursions by the dark forces who sought to enslave them. The light created in us the ability to use free will in a way that gave us each a choice over good and evil, as long as our souls were clean. We who walked in the light received gifts of magic and power that enabled us to meet our otherworldly adversaries on an even footing."

Quinn stopped him. "I don't know what people usually say when you tell this story, Clark. Even with everything

I've seen in the last day, I'm reluctant to believe this is all some sort of fight between demons and angels."

"Not just demons and angels, Quinn. All sorts of supernatural beings have been brought into the battle over the years."

"What, like werewolves and vampires and things?"

"Exactly. The councilman was a Lycan, what you would call a werewolf, which is a type of shifter."

"So, all those so-called creatures of the night are real? That makes no sense. You said you sought to protect him. If he was some sort of monster, why would you do that? You're a hunter. Aren't you supposed to kill people like him?"

"Once that would have been true. Over the years, though, many of the supernatural creatures switched sides, seeing as how they were being used to fight a war for the dark. The work of the hunters became less necessary, and people forgot about the fight for the light and dark. The clans fell from prominence and eventually became a coalition of disparate family groups that worked in the shadows of a world no one believed in anymore."

"What does any of this have to do with me? I might concede the existence of magic or maybe some sort of strange super-science I don't understand." Quinn paused as something Clark had said earlier came back to her. "You said you were the last survivor of the hunter clans, or you thought you were."

Clark sighed. "I've been alone for such a long time. For twenty years, I've hidden and run and fought. I've carried on the battle as best I could, always trying to find out who it was that betrayed us. The purges took two years from start to finish. By the end, there were only a few of us left, living on the run from place to place. I didn't even know I was the last of my family until I couldn't find any of the others, at least not alive."

Quinn's hand drifted up to touch her amulet as she listened. "And you think I'm...what? A lost hunter or something? I'm not some sort of magical monster slayer."

"Why is that so hard to believe? You don't know anything about your parents. They could be anyone. They could have been related to me. *You* could be related to me."

Quinn snorted a laugh. "Seriously? So I should call you Uncle Clark?"

Clark seemed uncomfortable with the subject. He looked at something or someone who wasn't there out through the windshield for a few seconds before answering, "I think we can dispense with that."

"Look, I appreciate that you think there's something special about me. Special enough to attack me in my Jeep while I was driving. We could've both died because of what you did, by the way."

Clark shook his head. "Hunters are hard to kill. Centuries of protection magic, along with our amulets, have toughened us. We heal faster than other people, and it takes more trauma than a normal person can stand to cause enough damage to finish us off. We'd have both survived any ordinary accident that didn't decapitate us or end in a fiery explosion. Have you ever noticed you don't ever get sick, and you heal faster than your friends?"

Quinn thought back to her sophomore year in high school when she blew out her knee in a lacrosse game. The docs said she'd be out for eight or nine months.

She was back and cleared to practice in just over a week. The orthopedic specialist had said it must've been a glitch in the MRI recording system that swapped images with another patient before the diagnosis. Could it have been her hunter genes instead?

Quinn didn't recall being sick, not ever. She found it funny in elementary school when friends missed school because a stomach bug ran through the class over the course of a few weeks.

Clark just sat there studying her expression.

He smiled and nodded when she looked his way. "I'm right, aren't I. Based on your expression right now, I think you know it, too."

"So? It doesn't change anything."

He laughed aloud. "It changes everything, Quinn. It's proof you're a hunter, or at least have the background and skills to become one. You also know you've got a connection to the death of someone, and the loss of an innocent bothers you. That was why you came down here."

Clark shook his head before continuing, "Quinn, the man who died tonight was a person who's stood in the way of bad things happening around here. He was the leader of the supernatural community, and kept them from drifting toward the darkness that started moving in after the clans disappeared."

"What kinds of bad things?"

"Since the purges, I've had a theory and have been tracking a small group of missing hunters from each of the clans. They all disappeared just before the purges began. Once the attacks started in earnest, everyone initially thought the missing ones had been among the first to die. However, I started to run across traces leading to them over the last few years, long after they should've been dead and gone. I've found these hints here and there, telling me they not only survived but may have been instrumental in exposing and betraying the rest of us."

"Why would anyone do such a thing?"

Clark shrugged. "Power and greed, the same old human weaknesses. The other side offers a great many benefits to their acolytes and followers. They become endowed with great power. The flip side is, their masters don't tolerate failure. There are no second chances for those who follow the dark."

"And you think these rogue hunters are somehow behind the killing tonight? You know there was more than one. A dozen or so candidates went into the system with missions tonight."

Clark paused, taken aback by her revelation. "I'll have to check on that. I only know about the one you killed…"

"I told you, I didn't kill him."

"Fine, the one you were involved with killing. I was only protecting one person. I couldn't protect everyone, so I chose the most important leaders to keep an eye on. What you just told me has me worrying about who else was killed tonight."

Quinn shrugged. "I have no idea. We were all hired to test some sort of virtual reality training system. That's all I know. I went into the VR system, and the next thing I know, I'm chasing a werewolf down the streets of Baltimore. I had no idea it might be real until after I'd left work for the night."

"Just tell me everything you know. Don't leave anything out."

Quinn thought about her company orientation the week before. She and the other candidates had all signed nondisclosure agreements. Of course, that was before she'd realized that somehow VirSync had implicated her in a murder and seemed to be doing a whole lot more than just testing some sort VR training software.

"I will tell you what little I know. Nothing I thought was true this morning seems to match up anymore."

"That's fine. Just tell me. Perhaps I can make sense of it for you."

Quinn nodded. She started off slowly, explaining how she and Taylor had been offered jobs right after graduating from high school. She described the offer and the initial orientation and training, as well as the testing room and the strange loss of time that had occurred that evening.

Clark listened in silence, waiting through her numerous pauses, giving her ample time to gather her thoughts.

When she'd finished telling him everything she knew, right down to the description of Fergus' attack on the creature in the game, she stopped and stared at Clark. "This doesn't make any sense, does it? "

"Unfortunately, it makes a whole lot of sense, especially when I add it to things I already know. After the purges, the few of us who were left thought the demon masters behind the attacks would make their move right away. We prepared to fight to the end. When nothing happened, a few relaxed, assuming the danger had finally passed. They were picked off one by one, even as I warned them the attacks weren't finished.

Clark paused and rubbed the stubble on his chin. "This might be the information I've been searching for all these years."

"Why?" Quinn asked. "VirSync has been around for years, making video games and other electronics. It's a Baltimore success story. How could they have possibly been involved with these purges the whole time you were searching for answers?"

"Hiding in plain sight is a powerful strategy. It never occurred to me they were operating in the open that way, but it all makes sense now. It allowed them to move around right under my nose while I searched for clues in dark alleys and amidst the supernatural community."

"I don't understand something," Quinn said. "Why didn't they move in and take over right away? You think they waited this long on purpose?"

Clark nodded. "It's the long game."

"What does that mean?"

"We humans perceive things in the small, bite-sized chunks of time that make up our puny lives. However, the plans of light and dark are grandiose and span years, decades, or even centuries. After destroying the bulk of the clans, the demons might have been free to begin the next phase of their plan, but there's no way they killed off the best trained supernatural fighters in the world without taking significant losses. After that, they needed to recuperate and regroup. It isn't easy for demonkind to manifest physically here on Earth, and it could easily have taken several decades for them to rebuild the power needed to enact the next part of their plans."

"Assuming this conspiracy theory you have about evil demons and the grand visions of light and dark are true, what does this have to do with me or anyone else? Why send us out through some VR game interface to kill someone in real life? Wouldn't it be easier to just hire a hitman or something?"

"If what you say is true, Quinn, they've devised an untraceable system that allows them to send a trained assassin virtually anywhere. They've proven it works, and it makes me wonder if any other recent deaths in the city or elsewhere in the world in recent months can be attributed to others like you. It's ingenious, actually."

"How so?"

"In addition to using you and your fellow candidates to eliminate those who stand in their way, they achieve an alternative goal as well. By tricking you into taking inno-cent human lives, they cause you to taint your souls, adding a dark price to the balance of your lives. Consider it a checkmark against you. Once there are enough check-marks in the black, they can use it to subvert your will or worse using their dark demonic rites."

"What do you mean? Some sort of demonic possession?"

Clark's grim nod sent a chill down Quinn's spine.

He continued after seeing her reaction, "I know it sounds crazy. I told you it took a lot of power or magical juice for a demon to manifest here in person. However, for a lesser expenditure, they can send their awareness into a sufficiently tainted soul. The more tainted the soul, the easier the possession. While not as powerful as being here in person, it offers the advantage of being harder to detect until they reveal themselves. One of our tasks as hunters before the purges was to rescue those in danger of such subversion and bring them back to the light by cleansing them of the darkness that put them at risk."

Quinn considered what he'd said. When he mentioned the risk to someone who had a confirmed kill, her thoughts turned to Taylor. She'd killed in the game that evening. If what he said was true, she'd broken her soul somehow.

"I have to get home. I have to see if Taylor's gotten back yet. She's in danger, and I need to help her."

Clark shook his head. "You aren't going anywhere but with me. It's not safe. You're completely untrained, and it's only through the most basic of your inherent abilities that you've been able to resist enough to see what really happened."

"Resist, how?"

"That has to be the source of the residual magic I smell on you. My guess is they're casting pretty powerful spells on you and your fellow candidates to ensure no one does exactly what you ended up doing. They can't afford for any of you to figure out the killing is real.

"Your amulet and your personal defenses broke through the spell halfway through the hunt for the were-wolf. That was why you could see the man in his human form. The others couldn't see that."

"Well, if that's the case, I have nothing to worry about. The amulet will protect me."

"Quinn, I can't guarantee it'll work for you again. Plus,

if they send you in for another mission, are you going to kill for them, just to stay close to your friend?"

"Of course not." The question shocked her, not because he asked it, but because she knew she'd do a lot to help her friend. She owed Taylor everything.

As she considered Clark's question, Quinn knew she'd lied. She would definitely kill if it meant she could rescue Taylor.

"What if I kill one of them, one of the people from this demon cult? Will that injure my soul too?"

"No, they're not innocents. Your kill would be applauded by the light and would accrue to you that way."

"Good, then I'm going back. I'm not abandoning Taylor. She's my best friend. Look, I probably won't have to go back in there. I just need to go home and talk her into quitting. Then you can clean her up or whatever you do."

"It's not an easy process, Quinn. A lot depends on the state of mind of the person involved."

"Good, then it's settled." Quinn tried her door again, and looked back at Clark. "I need to leave. Get out of my Jeep and let me go."

For a few long seconds, Clark didn't say anything. He just studied her face. "You're making a mistake. I can't protect you from a distance and your lack of training is a liability, especially now that you know a little of what is going on. You know enough to get into real trouble without being able to defend yourself."

"I shouldn't have to. Taylor will be home tonight if she isn't there already. I'll warn her to stay away, and then we'll come find you."

"What if she doesn't listen to you? Will you promise not to go back inside the company complex?"

"If I do go back, I'll be careful. Look, is there a way I can contact you?"

"Hand me your phone. I'll give you a contact number where someone will know how to get hold of me. It's the best I can do for now. I'll do some research into VirSync and its owners in the meantime. See what I can learn from the outside."

Clark tapped a number into her phone and handed it back to her. "Quinn, you need to understand that this is deadly serious work. If you go back in there alone, there's an even chance you won't come back out."

"My mind is made up. I need to do this."

Quinn tried the door again. Still locked. She glared at Clark.

He waved his hand again with two fingers raised, drawing something invisible in the air. Quinn's door unlocked.

"Thank you." Quinn opened the passenger door and hopped out.

Clark got out of the driver's side and held the door for her. "Don't thank me. This is against my better judgment. You may have just signed your own death warrant."

She answered with a curt nod and started the engine, then backed out of the spot. The headlights shone on Clark at the edge of the trees for a few seconds as she drove off. By the time she checked her rearview mirror, he'd disappeared into the darkness.

CHAPTER NINE

Quinn's mind whirled with more questions than answers as she drove back to her apartment after her encounter with Clark. Had she really found a connection to her parents? No one had ever been able to give her more than educated guesses about the runes and symbols on her pendant.

Plus, she now had proof that magic was real and not just some little girl's fantasy in the midst of a hard world. The memories of the secret warnings her amulet had given her dated back to when she was very young.

And what about Clark?

He'd held a knife to her throat. Under normal circumstances, she would have called the police to report him as soon as he let her go.

Except she couldn't, not without drawing a connection between herself and the councilman's murder. She was a witness to the crime, if not an accessory.

Quinn's hand balled up in a fist and thumped on the steering wheel. She was too wrapped up with this whole twisted and fantastical series of events. If even part of what Clark thought was going on at VirSync was true, all the candidates were in danger of…

Of what?

The eternal damnation of their souls? Possession by demons?

Quinn shook her head and tried to clear her thoughts. It was one thing to have your childhood belief in the existence of magic confirmed. It was another to believe you were the lost child of magical hunters, that demons existed, and possession by them was real.

Except everything Clark had told her lined up with all the strange things she'd encountered earlier that evening. While it didn't explain all the details of what happened to her and the others, the information she'd gleaned from him made more sense than anything she'd come up with.

There'd be time to sort out the truth of everything she'd learned from Clark later.

For now, Quinn had to focus on making sure Taylor was safe. That girl was a trouble magnet. She often got lost in the nerdiness of things and missed what was going on around her.

Once Quinn convinced Taylor of the truth, they could start planning their next steps.

Quinn got home and pulled into the building's parking lot. She locked the Jeep and looked up, locating their apartment window on the third floor.

The light was on.

A wave of relief washed over her. Taylor was home.

Quinn raced inside the building and headed up to their apartment, only to find it empty when she burst inside.

Her roommate wasn't there. They must've left the lights on when they'd left that morning.

Quinn cursed aloud. She must still be out with those programming friends she'd met.

Pulling out her phone, Quinn tapped a message to Taylor.

Where r u? Lights were on but u weren't here!

The response came back right away.

Coding marathon. Can't talk.
Don't wait up.

Quinn groaned and stomped around the apartment while she tried to think. She wouldn't see her roommate until morning.

Taylor probably wouldn't even answer any more texts. That girl would be lost inside some sort of computer world with her new geek friends for the rest of the night.

Quinn's anger wound down after a few minutes. She stopped and yawned, reaching up with both arms and arching her back to stretch. She needed sleep, and since there was nobody to talk to right now, it was the only thing that would settle her mind. It had been a long day, and everything she'd been through had left her thoroughly exhausted.

Kicking off her shoes, Quinn padded across the living room carpet into her bedroom, stripping down to a t-shirt and panties before climbing into bed. Maybe a good night's sleep would help her mind sort everything out.

As she drifted to sleep, she rested her fingertips on the edge of her pendant, which was nestled against her collarbone as she lay on her side. The hunter amulet was the key that tied everything together.

Her parents, both apparently killed long ago by the people she now worked for, must have hoped it would provide protection for her while she grew up alone. She tried to picture them, striving for a distant memory of a voice, a face, or anything, just as she had all her life. It was no good. Deep down, Quinn knew she was far too young to remember them.

She tried anyway, and fell asleep a long time later.

CHAPTER TEN

The buzz of a text message woke Quinn up to a room filled with bright sunlight.

Since we have to be at work at 4 anyway, Claire and Gary offered to let me hang at their place. We're going to play games online until we have to leave.
Don't worry, we won't be late.
I'll see you there.

Quinn shook her head as she sat up in bed and looked at the top of her phone to see what time it was.

It was nearly one in the afternoon.

Quinn shook her head as she tapped out a reply.

I need you to come home. Now. 911.

The reply came back right away.

Wrapped up in a major quest scenario right now.

You'll survive.
Tell me at work later.

Quinn snarled in frustration.

Need you now, not later.

She waited several minutes for an answer as she got up and went to make some breakfast, or lunch, or whatever it was at this time of day.

As time stretched, Quinn knew Taylor wasn't going to respond. She'd already returned to whatever game they were playing.

The cinnamon toast tasted like cardboard. Quinn realized she would have to return to VirSync. She had no choice. She had to persuade Taylor to quit before something horrible happened to her.

Quinn resigned herself to putting together a plan to get Taylor out. She'd convince her friend to feign being sick or something so they both could leave work before the evening's planned VR journey.

She couldn't let Taylor go back in and log another kill.

As her mind ticked through the possible options to get away once she explained things to Taylor, a part of Quinn's naturally curious mind also wanted to figure out exactly what was going on at VirSync. Clark had offered possibilities based on what he knew the other side capable of.

That wasn't good enough for her. Quinn wanted concrete proof that what the old man had told her was true. She wasn't sure she had to see a demon in the flesh to believe, but she needed something, some evidence, to back up his story.

The plan she eventually came up with offered solutions to both things she wanted to accomplish. She settled on an idea to head into work a little early on the pretense she was there to work out before the sessions began.

During orientation, all of the candidates had been told about a gym with a weight room and other workout equipment open for all the candidates to use twenty-four hours a day. Quinn decided to use that as cover for showing up a few hours early.

Maybe if no one else was around, she could try to search for evidence about what was happening behind the scenes with the VR system. If there were really magical spells or demons there, Quinn should be able to find something to back it up.

With her mind made up, she dressed in shorts and a t-shirt, shoved a change of clothes into her duffle bag, and headed down to her Jeep. She toyed with the idea of calling Clark and leaving a message for him about what she planned to do.

In the end, Quinn decided that was a bad idea. The number she had wasn't a direct line to Clark, just a place to leave a message for him. She had no idea who else would see the message. Besides, if she got him on the line, he'd only try to talk her out of it.

Traffic was light since it was a few hours before the afternoon rush hour. Twenty minutes later, Quinn pulled up to the gates at VirSync. Showing her badge to the guard, Quinn smiled despite the nervous pit in her stomach. He waved her through without a second thought, opening the heavy iron gate with the flick of a switch in the guard shack.

Quinn parked under the same overhead light as the night before and headed inside the main entrance with her bag slung over her shoulder.

Stopping again at the front desk, she smiled at the woman seated behind it. Quinn wondered if she knew she worked for a bunch of demon-worshiping cultists.

"Hey, I was told there's a weight room here somewhere, but I wasn't shown where it was. I thought I'd come in and get some reps in early."

The woman nodded as she scanned the badge clipped on Quinn's t-shirt. "It's in the same wing as your unit. Head down the way you normally go to your area. Follow the blue line this time, and it will lead you farther down that same hall, past where you'd turn off to go to the locker rooms."

"Thanks, I appreciate it." Quinn smiled and headed over to the double doors on the right side of the lobby. She followed the same path she had taken the day before, following both red and blue lines until the blue line separated from the red one.

She glanced behind her. No one else was in sight, and she kept going. Quinn was nervous, although she had every right to use the gym down here. She hadn't done anything wrong...yet.

Quinn continued down the corridor, following the blue line. At the very end of the hall, she stopped, facing a glass door through which she could see treadmills, stair climbers, and other cardio equipment. A full set of free weights and resistance equipment sat off to one side.

Ordinarily, Quinn would be impressed and excited to see such a well-equipped gym available for her use. She enjoyed staying in shape.

This time, though, she had other reasons for being here. She glanced to her left, where a steel door offered her access to the other floors and areas of the building.

Perfect.

She smiled and turned to reach for the stairwell door, only to find Phillip Ruiz standing just a few feet away. Where the hell had he come from?

"Phillip, you startled me."

"I'm so sorry. I saw that you had logged in at the front desk and was curious why you were here so early. I see you found our weight room."

Quinn nodded, hooking a thumb over her shoulder. "I'm kind of thinking I need to get some training in. You know, since I missed getting that kill yesterday. I thought perhaps I could work out a little before the testing session later this evening. I always perform better when I'm warmed up."

Phillip didn't answer right away. He paused for a few seconds, meeting her eyes as if searching for her real intentions.

Quinn held her ground and didn't blink. Clark had seen through her lies, but she hoped Phillip didn't see through her story as easily as the hunter had.

After an awkward pause, he nodded. "I think that's a very good idea. You should get in there and do that. I have to say, Quinn, it's good to see you putting in extra effort after your substandard performance yesterday. I expect you to show as much vigor in your mission inside the system later. We've got quite a chase set up for you and the others."

"Thank you. I promise I've got a lot more drive in me now than yesterday."

Phillip turned and headed back up the hall.

Quinn waited a few seconds, then pulled open the door to the workout room. She pretended to dig through her bag with the door held open by her foot until Phillip turned down the side hall toward the testing rooms. While she waited to make sure he didn't come back, Quinn ran through her options.

The upper floors were likely filled with the normal daytime staff and she wouldn't have an excuse to be up there, especially dressed as she was. She decided instead to head down to the lower level.

Quinn remembered one of the company engineers in her orientation describing the extensive equipment downstairs that ran the sophisticated virtual reality system the candidates would be testing. That would be a good place to start looking for answers. Maybe they kept records of some sort there, too.

Letting the glass door of the weight room close, Quinn checked the hall one last time before slipping into the stairwell.

She stopped inside the door to see if anyone came. She worried about how Phillip had snuck up on her undetected up in the hallway. It was strange, almost the same way Clark had surprised her in the Jeep or suddenly disappeared the night before as she drove away. It could've been magic like the amulet Clark had, or Phillip might just walk quietly, and she didn't hear him approach.

Quinn shook her head. She had to relax, or she'd never get anywhere. This whole thing was driving her crazy. How was she supposed to figure out what was real and what was magic?

She headed down to the basement level, where she stopped to listen at the door. She didn't hear a thing. She pressed her fingertips to the amulet beneath her T-shirt, focusing on it. Maybe it would warn her if there was trouble on the other side.

Quinn didn't know what to expect. Whatever it was, the silver oval didn't so much as twitch, or change in any way.

That was no help.

Taking a deep breath, she pulled open the door, revealing a long corridor with numerous steel doors on either side. At the far end was a large door with a window in the upper half. A short alcove branched off to the left, leading to an elevator.

Quinn checked the doors as she walked down the hall. Most were empty closets or storage rooms with shelves full of closed cardboard file boxes. A few were locked, and her keycard didn't open them.

Near the elevator alcove, one door opened to a small room lined with clothing hooks on the walls and a horizontal rack in the center like a walk-in closet. Hanging on the rack and walls were dozens of identical black cloaks or robes with red satin linings. She wondered what they were for.

Quinn continued down the hallway, passing the elevator alcove. She noted there was only an up button on the wall next to it. This must be the lowest level of the building.

Eventually, Quinn reached the end of the passage. She couldn't see much through the glass in the top half of the door. The room on the other side was dark.

She could make out a door on the opposite side of the room. She also saw what looked like four large tables in the center. One of the tables in the far corner had something on it, but Quinn couldn't tell what it was.

Disappointed at not finding much of interest down here, and certainly nothing that explained or verified anything Clark had said, Quinn sighed. She'd check out this last room and then head upstairs and work out in the gym while she waited for Taylor to arrive.

Quinn tried the door, finding it unlocked. She went inside, fumbling for a light switch to help her see more than just the shadowy shapes she'd already made out.

Finally, her fingers brushed a light switch, and she flicked it upward. The overhead fluorescent lights flickered on, illuminating a room with sterile tile walls and floors.

Four large wheeled stainless steel tables filled the center of the room.

The light also revealed what was on the table in the far corner.

A naked guy was laid out on the table like in a morgue. There was something black smeared all over his body in strange patterns. Quinn thought it was a manikin until she spotted his chest move with regular breaths.

As she drew closer, she made out more details. His whole body was covered in black letters and shapes drawn in ink or maybe paint. He hadn't moved, other than the shallow rise and fall of his chest.

Quinn spoke, trying to explain her presence. "Oh, sorry, I didn't mean to disturb you." Her voice quavered as she spoke. She went back to the door and started to flip the light off again.

She stopped when the man on the table still didn't move a muscle.

"Um, excuse me? I'm sorry to disturb your nap."

Nothing.

Quinn let her hand drop to her side as she took a few steps back toward the man, intrigued by the writing all over his naked body.

The symbols covered every inch of him, even his eyelids. They appeared to be geometric shapes, along with runes of some kind. None of them resembled numbers or letters in any alphabet she knew.

As Quinn stared at his face through the strange writing, she realized she knew this guy. He and another candidate named Jared from a previous test group had come in and talked to Quinn's group during their orientation. She couldn't remember this guy's name. He'd come into the company maybe a month or two before her arrival.

The question was, what was he doing here asleep, naked, and covered in this strange artwork?

Quinn worked up her courage and reached out after a few seconds, shaking his shoulder gently. When he didn't stir, she used both hands and jostled him more vigorously.

Still no response.

As Quinn struggled with what to do next, distant voices drifted down the hallway behind her. Realizing she couldn't retreat the way she had come without being seen, she tried to remain calm as she looked for someplace to hide.

A row of low cabinets ran along the wall to her left, with a long counter atop them. Quinn raced over and opened several of the bottom cabinet doors, relieved after three tries to finally find one of them empty.

Getting down on her hands and knees, she scrambled to jam herself inside the space. Quinn folded herself nearly in half and pulled the door closed with her fingertips, leaving it open just enough for her to peer out through the crack at the room.

She'd managed to hide just in time. Two people, a man and a woman, entered. Both wore the long black robes Quinn had seen in the room farther up the hallway. Although the robes had broad hoods, also lined in red satin, they didn't have them up, so she could see their faces through the crack.

Quinn stilled her excited breathing to listen.

The woman spoke as she entered. "So, we are supposed to be prepared to manage the transfer for how many of these newer candidates?"

"Myles said the new batch of candidates was even more promising than the first."

"They'd almost have to be, wouldn't they? Of the original ten, five were fired as unsuitable, and three more went insane and had to be disposed of. Only this guy and one other ended up completing their requisite two kills."

"Apparently, the new updates to the system, along with tweaks to the mind-control spells cast during VR immersion, fixed the issues they had. Did you hear that one of them even managed to get two kills his first session?"

The woman nodded as they stood next to the table with the naked candidate on it. "I assume he'll be the next one for the transference ritual?"

"That would be my guess. He's going to go back in tonight, but then he's scheduled to be rewarded for his efforts." The man let out an evil little chuckle as he continued, "I'll bet it sucks to be the one who missed their target and gave him the opportunity."

"So, only one of the missions failed with this batch? That's certainly an improvement. Did they fire the one who failed?"

"No, she apparently shows particular promise, and it was determined they'd give her another chance at success. I heard from Velma that there was some unexplained glitch in the system that must've screwed up her control and masking spell. She and Phillip have plans to strengthen the spell to exert more control on the next try."

The woman shook her head, her brow furrowed in concern. "How many do they expect to bring down for the rites over the next few days, then?"

"I'd guess at least the guy with two kills. He'll have three or more by the end of the night. Perhaps one or two others if they get kills during tonight's missions. There aren't as many targets available, so they'll be competing for the privilege."

"I don't know how they expect us to keep up the pace," the woman snarled. "The Ruby Heart needs to recharge between rituals, or the transfers won't take, and the subjects will eventually expel the spirit of the netherworld overlord inhabiting them."

The man shrugged. "What do I know? I'm just supposed to prep them. Make sure all the runes are in place and correctly spelled out so the transfer can occur. They successfully completed the transference on that Jared guy yesterday. Now that they know for sure it works with at least two kills on their souls, surely they can complete the others. Why don't you know? You're the one on track to become a high priestess."

The woman mumbled something Quinn couldn't make out, and the guy laughed.

The two turned to regard the comatose body on the table.

The woman pointed at the guy's chest. "What's that? Is that your idea of a joke?"

"Yeah." The guy chuckled. "I got bored and decided to add that rune for fun. What do you think?"

"Isn't that the rune for bloodlust?"

The man nodded. "This one's going to be a butcher if he ever gets the chance to make a kill while possessed. It'll let the worst of the demonic penchant for carnage leak through his persona. That should make for interesting times, don't you think?"

An evil grin crossed the woman's face. "I just hope the boss doesn't see it. He doesn't like it when you improvise."

"He never pays attention to the runes," the man said, waving his hand, dismissing the woman's concern. "By the time this guy gets to Myles, the ritual will be in full swing, and everyone will be focused on their chanting and the Ruby Heart."

"I hope you're right. I'm not taking the fall if it comes down to finding out who did that."

"You'd rat me out?"

"In a heartbeat. But that's on you now. It's too late to change the runes before the ritual of transference happens. Come on, let's wheel him out of here and get him down to the caverns so he's ready to go for the ceremony later."

They each gripped one end of the table, unlocking the wheels and rolling him toward the door opposite the one Quinn had entered through.

A keypad and card access point on the wall by the door lit up as the woman pulled out her badge and swiped it. The door popped open, and they wheeled the table with the naked guy out of the room and down what looked like another passage.

Quinn climbed out of her hiding place as soon as they had left the room and ran over to try to reach the door before it closed. She'd caught a glimpse of the hall that lay on the far side as they opened the door and passed through, but she wanted to know more about what lay on the far side.

Just before her hands reached the door, it clicked closed, and the lock reengaged. She carefully checked the handle just to be sure, but the door didn't budge.

Quinn considered everything she'd heard. It all but confirmed Clark's suspicions about what might be going on with the candidates. If he was right, they intended to invite some sort of demonic creature or spirit to take over that guy's body.

It also meant she, and especially Taylor, were in grave danger. If Taylor managed to make another kill in tonight's test session, she could be up for a trip to this mysterious ritual too.

Quinn moved to the other door, checking the window to make sure the corridor was clear before pushing it open. She raced back down the basement hallway and entered the stairwell.

She checked the time. The other candidates would begin arriving soon. She needed to get back upstairs and try to catch Taylor in time to talk her into going home before the testing began.

She hoped her friend listened to reason for once.

CHAPTER ELEVEN

No sooner had Quinn arrived back on the main level than a voice called to her from farther up the hallway.

"You there. What were you doing in that stairwell? That area is supposed to be off-limits for candidates."

Quinn froze for an instant, her mind racing for an answer. Plastering a smile on her face as she turned around, Quinn said, "I'm sorry. I needed to work out, and honestly, the stair climber in the gym is crap. I get a much better workout running actual steps, so that's what I've been doing. I didn't go anywhere else, honest."

The woman who called to her approached. Quinn didn't know her name, but she recognized her as one of Phillip's and Velma's colleagues. She was a test monitor for another of the candidates.

The woman scowled. It was clear she didn't believe what Quinn had said.

"Is it time to get ready for the next test session already?"

Quinn asked, keeping up her story. Maybe she could bluff her way past this woman's suspicions.

"That's still a half-hour or so away. I want to know what you're doing here so early."

"I told you, I'm here to work out. I screwed up yesterday and didn't get my kill. Phillip told me to work harder, and I figured a workout beforehand to loosen me up couldn't hurt. I'm hoping it'll help me be more focused the next time. I talked to him when I got here. You can ask him if you don't believe me."

The woman nodded but didn't seem convinced. She appeared to consider something before she raised her right hand in front of Quinn's face and made a strange gesture, as if drawing a symbol in the air. She murmured the word "truth" while staring into Quinn's eyes.

The amulet on Quinn's chest grew bitingly cold. She'd never felt it react this strongly before, but she had little doubt the woman had just tried to use some sort of magic on her. Realizing what the woman was trying to do to her from the word she uttered, Quinn let her eyes glaze over as she focused on the wall just past the woman's head. She let her mouth fall open a little, too.

The woman nodded. "Tell me what you were really doing. Don't lie to me."

Quinn answered in a monotone, "I don't want to fail again. I came in to work early so I could work out and show I was willing to get better. I hate being embarrassed."

There was a long, uncomfortable pause. Quinn resisted the urge to shift her eyes to the left to try to read the woman's expression. She knew that would give her away instantly.

Instead, Quinn focused on the plain white wall and tried to hold very still.

The woman let out an exasperated sigh. "Come with me. I know it's early, but we might as well get you prepped for today's session. I want to keep an eye on you."

The woman grabbed Quinn's upper arm and led her down the hall. Quinn tried to play up the act, shuffling her feet as she allowed herself to be steered back toward the entrance to the test wing.

Quinn knew she had taken a chance. She had no idea what someone under this kind of spell acted like.

She got the answer she'd feared soon enough. She found out she hadn't gotten it quite right when they reached the locker room. Another of the monitors, a man this time, was coming down the hall as they got to the women's locker room door.

The woman with Quinn waved the man over. "Jack, come here. Have you seen Phil Ruiz? I found this one in the stairwell by the weight room. She says she's one of his."

"No, but knowing what happened yesterday and the chewing out he got from the boss, he and Velma are probably double- and triple-checking the system and control spells in their room before tonight's mission."

He turned to consider Quinn, who tried to keep the vacant focus in her eyes without looking anywhere in particular. "You said she was in the stairwell? Had she been in the basement?"

"I have no idea. She claims to have been running up and down the steps instead of using the cardio equipment in the gym."

"Well, she shouldn't have been in there, no matter what

she was trying to do. It looks like she's compliant enough now. You charmed her?"

The woman nodded. "I used a truth charm. I can't shake the feeling she's resisting my spell somehow, though. She's answering me and following instructions, but I don't know. Something isn't right."

"Do you want to try a joint mind-control spell?"

The woman nodded. "I think that would be a good idea, just to be sure. I don't know why, but I don't trust her."

"If she's Phil's, then she's the one who screwed up yesterday. That makes her his problem. I don't want to use up my energy to cast something he should do."

"I don't either, but I've got things of my own to attend to, and it shouldn't take much power together to be sure. Then I can leave her here to get ready without worrying about her wandering around."

"Oh, very well. Let's get this over with. Phil's going to owe me, though." The man came closer to stand next to the woman, and the two of them turned to face Quinn. Both raised their right hands, making nearly identical gestures as they muttered words under their breath.

Quinn couldn't quite make out the words this time, so she didn't know how to react.

It didn't matter.

All of a sudden, Quinn found herself having a sort of out-of-body experience. She could still see and hear everything that was going on, but she was unable to control her body or her voice anymore. She felt it the instant her control was wrested away by the joint spell. The amulet blazed ice-cold against her chest, but it didn't remain that way.

This time, the silver charm was unable to completely defeat the power of the dual spell casters, and she found herself under the physical control of the two magic users. Quinn's gut wrenched as doubt about the wisdom of coming back here crashed over her.

"That seems to of done it," Jack said. "What do you think, Audrey?"

The woman nodded as well. "It seems like it took without much resistance that time. Did you feel anything?"

"I felt a slight pushback at the first stage of the spell, but it disappeared soon enough. She might just be naturally resistant."

"What, like a hunter? That's crazy. There aren't any hunters left."

"There could be a genetic component to the resistance, too. It doesn't matter, though. The spell clearly worked this time. Do you need me to stay here, or do you have this?"

Audrey nodded. "I've got her now. I'll take care of it."

The woman took Quinn by the arm and gave her a shove toward the women's locker room door. "Let's get you inside and changed. Whatever you've got going on, we're going to break you of it in the next testing session. Phillip and Velma won't tolerate anybody trying to put one over on them."

Quinn's body stiffened at the commands from the woman, and her legs moved to comply without any control from her mind. No matter how hard she tried, she couldn't stop or even slow herself. She walked into the locker room and over to the locker she'd used the day before.

"Get changed, then sit and wait here on the bench until

I return." Audrey delivered her order and headed back to the toilet stalls by the showers.

Quinn worked harder to force her will through the spell's control over her.

It was no use.

Without hesitating, Quinn undressed, folding her shorts and t-shirt and placing them on the locker's top shelf. Once she'd stripped down to her panties and sports bra, she removed the freshly laundered jumpsuit.

As she slipped into the skintight outfit, Quinn realized she still had her amulet around her neck. She could feel the slightly chilled metal against her chest as the jumpsuit pressed it to her skin. Quinn breathed a mental sigh of relief that Audrey had left the room while she dressed. The woman didn't see the hunter amulet or ask her to remove it.

Quinn continued to fight for control as she shut the locker, setting the lock with her thumbprint. She walked over to the bench, where she sat facing the far wall, waiting obediently for the woman's return.

Audrey sported a satisfied grin as she returned to the dressing area to find Quinn sitting and awaiting further instructions. "Well, that's better. You are to sit here until the other candidates arrive and begin dressing. Once one of them leaves the locker room for the next VR session, you may leave as well. You are to go directly to your test chamber and check in with Phillip and Velma. I will advise them of my suspicions. I'm sure they will have more to say to you after I've talked to them."

Quinn remained on the wooden bench in front of the lockers, her back rigid, her eyes locked on the far wall. The woman gave a brief chuckle, then left Quinn alone in the locker room.

As soon as she departed, Quinn redoubled her efforts to free herself. She tried everything she could think of.

Nothing worked.

She failed to move even a finger as she sat there. The magic the two spell-casters had used on her remained in complete control. It could have been worse. She was pretty sure they had meant to control her thoughts and memory as well, which meant she'd resisted the spell in part. Still, she was forced for now to comply with Audrey's orders until the spell wore off or something changed.

Quinn continued to try with desperate futility to regain control of herself. By the time she'd waited the half-hour it took for the other candidates to begin to arrive, she was mentally exhausted.

Taylor came in with a group of other candidates to get changed. She spotted Quinn sitting on the bench and came over right away.

When Quinn didn't even glance in her direction, Taylor said, "Hey, judging from the look on your face and the silent treatment, I guess you're a little pissed off with me for blowing you off when you texted me earlier. I'm sorry. Claire and Gary are really fun to hang with, and we were in the middle of a super-hard quest. You know what that's like."

Quinn struggled to force words from her mouth, but she couldn't say anything. She could only stare up at Taylor from where she sat.

After a few seconds, Taylor let out an exasperated grunt. "Fine, I was trying to apologize for bailing on you. If you're not going to talk to me, I guess we'll just have to leave it there. Maybe you'll change your tune after the VR session."

Taylor spun, flipping her hair with a dramatic twist of her head, and went over to her locker, where she dressed in her jumpsuit for the next session.

A few minutes later, the first group of girls headed out of the locker room. The woman's commands took over again, and she followed them out.

When she reached her testing room, Quinn pulled open the door and entered the outer control room, where Phillip and Velma waited.

Phillip smiled when she walked in. "Ah, look who's here. Audrey told us she had to cast a reinforcement spell on you after you resisted her attempts to question you."

Velma chuckled from where she sat at the desk behind the computer equipment. "Audrey's a paranoid bitch, Phil. You know that."

Phillip shook his head. "Maybe, but after the issues we had with last night's session, it's best to leave the compulsion spell in place for now."

He turned to Quinn and pointed to the door leading into the main testing room with the VR gear. "Go ahead and get yourself ready for the session. You'd better not screw up this time, Quinn. I expect a kill from you, or we're going to have some major questions for you when you come out of the mission."

Quinn headed into the test room, following Phillip's instructions to the letter. She sat down on the VR exam couch, picked up the headset, and lowered it over the crown of her head. Once it was in place, she lay back, staring at the ceiling and waiting for Phillip's order to lower her visor.

Something different happened in the sequence this time, though. Phillip came in and stood next to her. He lowered her visor for her, then began waving his hands as she'd seen the other two monitors do when they took control earlier.

He sketched shapes and figures in the air over her with two fingers outstretched on each hand. He muttered a chant under his breath at the same time.

Darkness started folding inward from the edges of her vision. Quinn struggled to keep listening and focus on retaining control, but a sudden, sharp pain stabbed through her mind as a mental yank at her consciousness pulled her away.

Phillip's chanting faded, and everything went black.

CHAPTER TWELVE

Quinn's eyes popped open.

She stood in a crowd of people. They moved around her, and a few even bumped into her as she stood at the curb near the corner of a busy city street.

A corner of her mind recognized the area. She was only a few blocks from Baltimore's Inner Harbor shopping district.

Quest orders for the mission rang clear in her mind as if she'd just read them. She and the other hunters were charged with tracking down a small group of evil magic users. According to the mission briefing, they used their mind-control spells to force victims to shift their bank accounts to the mages' control.

Quinn started moving to find her targets, then paused. Her orders were clear, and yet when she thought about her mission and the mind-control magic, something didn't ring true.

She shook her head, trying to clear her mind. On its face, everything seemed as it should be.

When she looked down at her outfit, it was her usual urban hunting gear. Jeans, t-shirt, black leather jacket, and black knee-high boots. With her left hand, she checked the placement of her Bowie. This time she wore it in a shoulder sheath for concealment, which hung hilt-down beneath her right arm inside the jacket, relying on a leather band that snapped in place to hold the blade in place.

Everything was as it should be, so why did she feel like it was all wrong?

Quinn considered her mission info again. There was only a loose description of the mages they hunted, but she wasn't worried. She had the distinct impression from the briefing info that if she got close enough, she'd know them.

She scanned the crowded sidewalk in both directions on her side of the street and spotted others from her hunter group, including Taylor, Fergus, and several others. They were spaced about fifty yards apart, with Quinn in the center. Judging from the way they all craned their necks, they, too, were searching the crowd for their quarry.

Turning her attention back to tracking down the targets, Quinn spotted a group of five people across the street on the opposite sidewalk. It took her a few seconds to understand why they stood out from the others hustling past them. The group stood back to back, arranged so one of them faced in every direction.

The crowd surged around them as the quintet held their ground. Then the group began moving away from her.

As they did, Quinn realized they all held hands as they slowly moved through the crowd.

A system message pinged her.

. . .

Targets acquired.

Quinn managed to catch Taylor's eye as her friend scanned the crowd. Quinn nodded in the direction of the quintet of mages. Taylor scanned the crowd for a few seconds and then nodded, a big grin crossing her face.

The other hunters noticed Quinn and Taylor crossing the street. There were five hunters, one for each of the targets.

They wouldn't escape, not now that the team of hunters had found them.

Quinn and the others moved in, speeding up to a fast walk and twisting and dodging as they worked their way through the crowd to approach the mage circle.

The three women and two men shuffled down the street away from the hunters. All looked young, perhaps in their twenties or early thirties, dressed like everyone else in casual attire.

They still hadn't noticed the approaching hunters, although their defensive arrangement showed they expected trouble.

Quinn smiled as she got closer. She saw all of their mouths moving and realized they must be casting some sort of a spell.

If it was a concealment and protection spell, it was a pretty poor one since the hunters had found them easily enough.

At the thought of protection magic, an icy-cold spot

pressed against the center of Quinn's chest. She started to reach for her t-shirt to see what it was, but shook it off as the sensation passed. Her hand dropped back to her side.

The hunters got closer. This was going to be easy. The mages still hadn't noticed them.

Quinn started to take another step forward, but something wrapped around her legs, and she fell to the pavement.

She pitched forward so suddenly that she barely caught herself before her head slammed into the concrete.

Wondering why it felt like someone held onto her legs, Quinn rolled to her side and looked down. Inch-thick green and brown vines twisted around her ankles, sprouting from a crack in the sidewalk.

Quinn growled in anger. The mages had spotted the hunters after all. She should have been more careful. It had been a foolish move on her part, one that might cost her a chance at her first kill.

Sitting up, Quinn drew her Bowie. She slashed and hacked at the vines even as they continued twisting around her legs, holding them together.

Quinn shifted her attack to focus on where they grew out of the sidewalk. This was taking too long. Her Bowie was razor-sharp. It shouldn't be having this much trouble with a few vines.

It took precious seconds she didn't have to hack through the tough stalks. The mages were getting away.

Once she cut the last of the vines at the base, they ceased tightening around her ankles. She managed to unwrap them, freeing her feet.

The nearby people walking about their daily tasks paid

no attention to the woman wielding a big knife and struggling with magical vines on the sidewalk. They merely walked around her, with only a casual glance in her direction.

Finally free, Quinn stood and scanned the crowd.

The cluster of mages had disappeared.

Quinn craned her neck to see above the heads of the people around her. There was no sign of them.

There was no sign of her hunter team, either. Had they already begun the chase and left her behind after she fell?

She got her answer when Fergus's head popped up above the crowd not far away.

Taylor's face appeared nearby, followed by the other two team members.

Quinn relaxed. They'd all been taken down by the same spell. The mages had spotted the team.

With a nod to the others, Quinn scanned the area ahead, looking for the mages again. Fergus, who was off to her right, shouted and pointed farther down the street.

Quinn looked that way, searching amidst the people walking in that direction. She picked out the circle of spell casters right away. They were moving a lot faster now, their circle broken as they dodged the other pedestrians.

"After them," Quinn shouted to the others, but the order was unnecessary. The rest of the hunters had started running down the street after the escaping targets.

This time, the mages didn't hide the fact they saw the hunters approaching. Eyes widened as five heads swiveled in their direction. Quinn readied herself to try to dodge any incoming spells.

When nothing came at the charging hunters, she wondered if they had any other spells to use.

Their escape plan must have changed because the circle broke apart, each ducking and disappearing into the crowd.

Quinn cursed and pressed onward. Other pedestrians hindered her progress as they hustled past, oblivious to the hunt. She eventually reached the location where the group had split up, and she turned in a circle to look for any signs of the missing mages.

Fergus and Taylor arrived next, scanning the crowd as they stopped beside Quinn.

"Where did they go?" Taylor asked.

"They can't have gone far," Fergus said. "Let's split up and move in different directions."

Quinn nodded. It was as good a plan as any.

She pointed to the right as the final two hunters joined them. "I'll go this way. See you all back at the training center."

The others laughed, enjoying the chase.

The five hunters wove through the crowd as they took off in different directions.

Quinn moved at a fast walk as she scanned the area ahead. As she did so, a new ability icon popped up in her HUD. Not recognizing the icon, she mentally clicked it as she kept moving.

A menu with a selection of things she could do popped up. One of them flashed brighter, indicating a new ability.

Tracking

. . .

Quinn wasn't sure how such a thing would work on a busy urban street, but it was as good an option as any at this point. She had no idea where any of the targets were.

Activating the tracking skill, Quinn waited to see what happened. She didn't see anything at first, but then she happened to glance down and spotted a thin, glittering golden trail weaving through the crowd ahead of her and angling to the left.

Quinn started to move along the trail, going slower than before as she tried to navigate the crowded sidewalk while following her targets. As she did, the golden thread began fading.

Realizing her quarry must be getting farther away, Quinn picked up speed.

She began jogging down the crowded sidewalk, weaving around people and then vehicles as she followed the trail across a busy street. She turned down another sidewalk perpendicular to the first until she reached a broad open area with a grassy field. It was a small park.

The crowd thinned out here, helping her keep the trail in sight. Quinn smiled and moved into the park. She stopped as she reached the grassy area.

Looking along the trail, she spotted one of the women mages moving at a fast walk.

The woman glanced behind her and must've spotted Quinn because she turned and bolted across the park toward a tall chain-link fence. As she approached the fence, which had to be over six feet tall, the woman waved her hands in a broad, sweeping gesture.

To Quinn's amazement, the woman took a last leaping stride and cleared the fence with ease. She landed on the far side and kept going without missing a step.

Quinn took off after the woman at a run. When she got to the fence and jumped, she reached up to grip the top of the fence and pulled herself up, bending at the waist over the top and swinging her legs over to follow the rest of her body.

On the way down the other side, Quinn twisted her body and landed on her feet in a crouch. The mage had widened the distance between them. She had already crossed the next street, running for her life.

Quinn knew the woman was headed toward a more crowded area of the city near the harbor. If she kept pulling away from Quinn, it would easier to evade pursuit amidst the people there.

The glittering tracking trail had nearly faded to nothing. A countdown timer appeared in her HUD, indicating that her tracking ability was running out.

Quinn brought up her stamina bar as she'd done the day before. Drawing on her stamina, Quinn drained twenty-five percent again and dropped the surge of extra power into her strength. Her legs moved faster as the additional strength manifested as speed. Once again, Quinn took off after her target.

Moving at double her normal speed, Quinn gained on the woman, finally catching up with her as she took a shortcut down an alley behind a street full of businesses.

The woman spotted Quinn and turned to face her attacker. She shouted, holding her hands out as she backpedaled, pleading for mercy, "No, please."

Quinn ignored her, diving forward and tackling her to the ground.

The woman grunted in pain as they landed.

A rush of air hit Quinn's face as the hard landing knocked the breath from the woman's lungs.

Quinn smiled. This was going to be so easy.

Straddling the mage's waist, Quinn reached inside her jacket to draw her knife. Raising the blade high over her head with both hands clenched around the hilt, she prepared to plunge it into the woman's heart.

Quinn would silence this evil mage forever.

"Please, stop," the woman's voice croaked out as she tried to regain her breath. "You don't have to do this. I'm not your enemy."

Quinn hesitated, slowing the descent of her knife.

Something in the woman's voice tickled a memory in the deep recesses of Quinn's mind. The memory hinted there might be some truth in her words.

Quinn shook her head, trying to clear the disconcerting thoughts. She had to get this kill, or she'd lose the incredible opportunity she had working at VirSync.

She raised the knife again. A stabbing cold in the center of her chest distracted her this time. Quinn took her right hand off the dagger's hilt and brought it down to her chest. What the hell was causing that pain?

Quinn's fingers traced the oval of a small disc of freezing cold metal beneath her shirt. She reached into her collar to pull out a thin silver chain, from which dangled a pendant etched with runes.

As soon as she saw it, her mind cleared. It was as if someone had pulled back the curtain hiding the truth.

Quinn was herself again, in complete control. She realized how close she'd come to killing this woman.

The woman beneath her regained her breath and voice. She shoved Quinn and shouted for help, almost dislodging herself from beneath her assailant.

Quinn sheathed her blade and leaned forward as she clapped her hand across the woman's mouth

"Hush. I'm not going to kill you."

The woman stopped struggling, but the wild fear in her eyes told Quinn she didn't believe her.

Well, Quinn thought, she wouldn't believe it either in the same situation.

"Look, I was under some sort of spell. Do you understand what that means? I didn't know what it was I was doing. I didn't remember who I really was."

The woman nodded.

"Good. I'm going to take my hand away. Don't scream. We don't want to draw attention to us. It's too likely one of my companions will hear you and come to investigate. I might not be able to stop them from killing you if that happens."

Once again, the woman nodded, and Quinn took her hand away.

The woman twisted her head to look up and down the alley. "How did you find us?"

"I'm not sure. Look, it's a long story. All I know is, I sort of woke up across the street from you and your friends."

"That doesn't make any sense. How could you wake up in the middle of a busy street corner like that?"

"I don't have time to explain it. Hell, I don't understand

it," Quinn said as she stood and helped the woman to her feet.

As the woman brushed herself off, Quinn looked back up the alley toward the main street.

Taylor came into view, walking down the sidewalk. She crossed the end of the alley.

Quinn ducked and pushed the mage into a gap between a building and a detached garage beside it.

It might be enough to hide them from view. Quinn peered around the corner of the garage.

Taylor kept walking without looking their way. Quinn watched her until she'd disappeared from sight.

"We've got to get out of here," Quinn said, turning back to the woman she'd pressed against the garage's cinderblock wall. Her mind spun through options to escape the other hunters.

The woman shook her head. "I don't know where to go. Clearly, you people can find me wherever I am."

An idea came to Quinn. "I have an idea about who we can turn to for help, but you have to trust me. Do you have a phone? I don't have mine with me."

The woman nodded and reached into her pocket, pulling out a phone and handing it to Quinn.

Taking the phone, Quinn crouched and struggled through her still-foggy mind to remember the number Clark gave her.

"Who are you going to call?"

"If I can remember his number, it's a friend who should be able to get us both out of this mess."

Quinn dialed, hoping there was a solution on the other end of the line.

CHAPTER THIRTEEN

Quinn waited while the phone rang on the other end. She hoped Clark picked up, even though he'd said it was someone else's number.

The line was answered, and Quinn's heart sank as she heard a woman's voice ask, "Who is it?"

"I don't have a lot of time. My name is Quinn Faust. I need to speak to Clark. It's urgent. Do you know him?"

"How did you get this number? Clark shouldn't have given it to you."

"He told me this was a way to get hold of him. Can you reach him or not?"

That was a brief pause. Quinn checked the alley's entrance again for any sign of Taylor or the others while she waited for an answer. After a few seconds, the woman finally answered. "I can. What do you want me to tell him?"

"Give him this number and tell him to call me back right away. It's a matter of life and death. "

"Fine."

The woman hung up.

The mage or sorceress or whatever she was crouched in the alley next to Quinn, wringing her hands. "So, what now?"

Quinn leaned forward again, looking up and down the alley for any of the other hunters. She kept up her lookout as she answered, "Now we wait for someone to call us back."

Quinn glanced at the detached garage beside them, then moved into the alley and tried lifting the metal garage door. It rattled when she yanked on it, but it didn't open.

She motioned for the other woman to follow her as she moved around to the garage's far side. There was a door there.

She tried the knob. Of course, it was locked.

"I can help with that," the woman behind her said. "Move over."

Quinn slid farther into the narrow space between the garage and the tall metal fence protecting the rear of the building next to this property.

The woman crouched until she was at eye level with the doorknob. She raised two fingers on her right hand and muttered a few quiet phrases while she twitched her fingertips a few times near the keyhole.

After a few seconds, she smiled and stood, turning the knob and opening the door to reveal the dark interior beyond.

"Neat trick," Quinn said. There were more than a few times in her past on the streets where that would have come in handy.

"It's not hard once you understand how locks work."

"Let's get out of sight while we wait for the return call. Get in there while I check the alley one last time."

The other woman sighed and stepped into the dark interior of the garage. Quinn checked to make sure the alley was still clear and then entered the garage, closing the door. Very little light filtered in through the single grimy window in the far wall. Like most garages Quinn had seen, it didn't contain a car. Instead, moldy cardboard boxes and stacks of broken furniture filled the space.

Quinn pulled a chair with a broken back off a stack nearby. It shifted a little when she settled her weight on it, but it held her.

She gestured to the pile. "Take a seat. We might be here a while."

"I'll stand if that's all right."

"Suit yourself."

After a full minute of awkward silence, Quinn glanced at the woman pacing by the door. "What's your name?"

"Miranda. I gather from the phone conversation your name is Quinn?"

Quinn nodded, noticing the scrapes on the woman's elbows. "I'm sorry if I hurt you. There's something going on here I don't understand yet. Some sort of magic clouded my mind and made me chase you. The good news is you're safe for now."

"What about my friends? We've been working on an important project together. We have to continue it."

Quinn shook her head. "I don't know. They have other people like me chasing them."

Miranda's eyes widened. "Hopefully, they'll all come to their senses like you did before anyone gets hurt."

Quinn's expression must have answered the other woman's question. Quinn quickly said, "Maybe your friends were able to lose the others in the crowd. They might already be safe."

There was another awkward pause as Miranda went back to pacing. She favored her right leg.

"Is your leg okay?" Quinn asked.

"I don't think anything's broken, but I'm pretty banged up. You try getting tackled onto concrete and have someone land on top of you. It's not pleasant, trust me."

The awkward tension between them and the matter-of-fact way she said it almost made Quinn laugh despite everything that was going on. She covered it with a cough and cleared her throat.

She was about to remark how the whole situation was crazy when Miranda's phone vibrated, signaling an incoming call.

Quinn tapped to pick up and put the phone to her ear. "Hello?"

"Quinn, is that you?"

Quinn let out a sigh. "Clark, thank God. I'm calling because I'm back inside the VR system."

"What? You were supposed to stay home and keep your friend there with you."

"That didn't work out, and then they used some kind of control magic on me, so I had to do what they asked me to."

After a spate of unintelligible grumbles from the other end, Clark said, "Where are you?"

"I'm in an alley between Fells Point and the Inner

Harbor. I have a woman here with me. She was my target for the mission."

"Is she all right?"

Quinn rolled her eyes. "I didn't kill her if that's what you mean. Look, I don't know how long I'll be here before they recall me from the VR system. What do I do? They're going to want a good reason why I didn't kill my target this time."

"All right, I think I know the area where you are. I've got an idea, but you've got to hurry because you've got some distance to go."

"What do we do?"

"Head east toward the waterfront. You'll come out between some warehouses next to a pier. I'll meet you there."

"What do we do when we get to the water?"

"I'll explain later. Take the woman with you and meet me there. Go now."

Clark hung up before Quinn could ask any more questions. She turned to Miranda. "He wants me to head east from here to some warehouses by the harbor. You're to come with me. Are you good with that?"

Miranda thought for a second, then nodded. "Yes."

"Good, then let's get moving. Let me go out and check to make sure none of the others are around."

Quinn stepped outside and looked both ways, then called to Miranda, "It looks like we're in the clear. Are you ready to run? As long as we keep moving, we should be able to stay ahead of the other hunters. Run when I run. Stop when I stop. Got it?"

Miranda nodded.

"Good, let's go."

Quinn and Miranda ran down the alley. Quinn stopped long enough to check the street, then the two of them darted across it into another alley that led toward the harbor's edge.

The alley ended in a tall wooden fence. Quinn slowed as she approached it to try to figure a way over. Miranda did the magic jumping thing again and vaulted to the top of the fence.

She reached down to help Quinn up.

Quinn laughed as she reached the top. "You have to show me how you do that, too."

"I'm not sure you'll be able to do that sort of magic, but if you can, and we live through this, I will."

Quinn smiled and jumped down to the lot on the other side. She and Miranda continued zig-zagging between buildings and alleys until they reached the dockside area Clark had described.

Miranda pointed across the street. "The water should be one block that way through the industrial park."

She started to step out from between the buildings where they hid, but Quinn hissed a warning and pulled her back into the shadows.

There, standing between two buildings across the street, was Taylor. Luckily, she'd turned away from them and scanning the area the street in the opposite direction.

"That's my friend, Taylor. We can't let her see us."

"What are we going to do? If she's there, the others are probably close, too. We don't have time to wait. Just fight her so I can get by."

Quinn shook her head. "If I fight her, she'll remember it when we get back."

"What do you mean when you get back? Aren't you coming with me?"

"No, I can't. Look, Miranda, it's a long story, but somehow, I'm not really here. I can't explain how, but they can sort of teleport us to places where they want us to hunt down people. All I know is that when they decide to pull me out, I'll simply wake up back there. We can't afford to have Taylor know I helped you. Even though she's my friend, I don't think she's acting of her own volition right now. They use magic to supplement the technology, and I think it has a mind-control component to it."

Miranda stared at Quinn and said, "I have so many questions about what you just said, but if it's true, you're right, we don't have the time. I can help solve your problem, though. I can do a short-term memory wipe. It's only good for clearing out about thirty seconds of memories, but if you can disable her in that timeframe, I'm pretty certain I can make it so she doesn't remember what happened."

Quinn didn't want to fight her best friend, but that was the only option they had to get across the street.

"All right, we'll do it your way. I'm going to run over to her. When I reach her, run after me. Have that spell ready. The sooner I disable her, the better. Then you do your mojo while I pull her out of sight between those warehouses. We'll leave her there until she comes around."

Miranda nodded, and Quinn turned to look up and down the street again. Then the hunter darted out of the shadows and ran straight across the street toward Taylor.

Taylor caught the movement and turned to face it, crouched and ready to defend herself. She had a short-bladed *tantō* in her hand.

She relaxed and waved when she saw Quinn. "Hey, I killed mine and came to help you. Where's the woman you were chasing?"

Quinn didn't answer, just continued toward her at full speed. When she reached Taylor, she tackled her to the ground. Taylor's knife skittered across the pavement.

Taking advantage of Taylor's stunned expression, Quinn pulled out her knife but shifted her grip so she brought the pommel down hard on the side of Taylor's head just in front of her ear.

Taylor shouted once, then her eyes closed.

Initially, Quinn thought she'd been successful.

A mere two seconds after her eyes closed, Taylor's eyes popped open again, and she swung a wild punch at the side of Quinn's head.

Wincing at both the strike to her head and what she had to do, Quinn realized she was going to have to hit her friend again. She batted away Taylor's flailing arms and managed to land another strike in at the same spot. This time Taylor's eyes rolled back in her head, staying closed as she fell silent and laid still.

"Stand up and step away from her," Miranda called as she ran up behind them.

Quinn got up, sheathed her Bowie, and moved away to stand next to the spell-caster.

Miranda once again traced signs in the air, waving her arms while she muttered, "Forget."

There was no visible change in Taylor.

Quinn looked at Miranda. "Well? Did it work?"

Miranda shrugged. "I hope so. We won't know until you get back. It should've worked, but if she's not here in her own body like you said, I don't know for sure."

Quinn wished she'd known about the woman's doubts before now. She reached down to drag Taylor into the shadows nearby.

There was a brief flash of light that left Quinn blinking in surprise at an empty spot on the pavement.

"Where'd she go?" Miranda asked.

"I guess when she lost consciousness, the VR system recalled her. I sure hope that spell worked, or I'm screwed when my turn comes."

Realizing it could happen to her at any moment, Quinn pushed Miranda toward the two nearby warehouses. "Go, I'm right behind you. When you get near the water, look for an old guy in a black trench coat. If you see anyone else, zap them or something. You can do more magic, right?"

Miranda shook her head. "We'd been casting all day. I might have enough juice left for one more spell."

"I'll defend you, but be ready with that forget spell if I call you over."

While Miranda started though the last stretch to the harbor, Quinn scanned the street behind them one last time. There was no one there, and Quinn turned to race after Miranda.

Five minutes later, the two of them stood at the edge of a pier, staring out at the water.

"Now what?" Miranda asked.

Quinn opened her mouth to answer but closed it when

Clark once again startled her with his surprise appearance trick. "Now you let me take it from here."

Quinn glared at him. "Stop that. It's not nice to sneak up on people. I could've killed you before I knew who it was."

Clark looked down at her and laughed. "You? Kill *me*? Not hardly."

He turned to Miranda and offered a slight bow at the waist. "Sorry I wasn't close enough to protect you and your coven, Milady. Hopefully the others survived as well."

"It is nice to see a hunter who still understands the proper forms," Miranda said. She cast a sideways glance in Quinn's direction. "Some of your people are a little rough around the edges."

"She's not my people, at least not officially. She's an interesting anomaly I recently discovered."

Quinn scanned their surroundings for the other hunters and pretended not to hear his remarks. After making sure it was still clear, she turned back to Clark and Miranda. "Look, I'm glad you two are having this reunion, but we need to get this figured out. They can pull me out of here any time."

"The plan is, you're going to tell them you chased her here, where she fell in the water and disappeared."

Quinn stared at Clark, trying to understand how this simple statement was going to solve anything. "That's it?"

Clark nodded. "You'll be credited with the kill, at least initially. If they examine you for the taint, it'll help explain why they can't detect a stain on your soul. They'll assume it was an accidental drowning, not attributed by the higher powers to you. It's the perfect answer, really."

Quinn wasn't sure. "If you say so. How are you going to get her away?"

"I can keep her hidden long enough to get us out of the general area. I'll take care of protecting her in a safe location while I try to find the others from her coven."

He eyed her, taking in her outfit. "Nice. Are you going to be able to get away when you get back?"

"I think so, now that I've got this cover story about the drowning."

"Well, there *is* one thing I can do to help you. I should've done it last night while we were together. Take out your amulet. I have something to show you."

Quinn did as she was told, holding it between her thumb and forefinger.

"One of the first protections an initiate learns is to conceal themselves from those who seek them. It's a useful skill, and given how attuned you've become to your amulet growing up, it shouldn't be a problem for you to learn it."

"What do I do?"

"First, this will work only as long as the amulet is touching your body. On the chain around your neck is fine, as long as it's touching skin. Got that?"

Quinn nodded.

Clark continued. "Find a shadow nearby, any shadow, and concentrate on it. In the beginning, you'll need a keyword to activate it. Eventually, you'll be able to do it without the word. Either way, you'll be able to sort of disappear. You're still there. It just makes it so people don't notice you. It won't work on everybody, especially anyone with magical abilities who knows you're there and looks for you, so be careful how you use it."

"What word am I supposed to use?"

"I used 'mist' when I was younger. Try that."

"That's it? I say 'mist,' and I'll just disappear from view?"

"It won't work in any sort of bright light, but if there are shadows nearby, you'll be able to fold them around you so you go unnoticed."

Quinn nodded, glancing down at her amulet before dropping it back inside her t-shirt. "You'd better get going. Taylor will probably wake up soon back at VirSync, and Fergus can't be far behind me along with the others. Go. I'll be fine."

Clark smiled and reached out for Miranda's hand. He glanced over his shoulder at Quinn, nodded, and started walking down the pier. As they moved away, they both slowly faded from sight. They were gone in less than five steps.

The instant he disappeared, shouts came from behind Quinn, and she spun around to see Fergus and the other two racing toward her from between two of the warehouses.

Fergus called to her, "Did you kill the witch? Don't tell me she got away from you."

"I got her, all right."

Fergus looked around as he approached. "Where's the body?"

She pointed to the harbor. "I chased and fought her all the way to the edge, but she went over, right into the water. I watched her struggle for a bit before she went under. She must've drowned. There's been no sign of her since."

Fergus laughed. "You didn't gut her with your knife first to be sure? That's pretty sloppy."

Quinn shrugged, trying to sell the story as best she could.

The two with him seemed doubtful too, but they let her story stand for now.

Fergus beckoned to the others and started back toward the warehouses. As they did, they winked out in a flash of light one by one.

After the last one disappeared, Quinn felt the familiar pull at her core, and darkness closed in around her as the system pulled her back to the testing room at VirSync.

CHAPTER FOURTEEN

Quinn jolted awake in the testing room. She lay there for a few seconds, staring up at the ceiling in the dim light through the VR visor's tinted glass.

She tried to lift her arms to remove the visor and head-gear, but nothing moved. For a panicked instant, Quinn thought she might still be trapped under the control spell from before the training session began. If that was the case, she'd be unable to lie about what had happened in the scenario.

Right before the outer door opened, she started getting feeling back in her arms and legs, much to her relief. Quinn slowly lifted the visor as she sat up and swung her legs over the edge of the exam table.

Phillip strolled in with a big grin on his face. "I got a text from one of the other monitors. Their candidate said you made the kill. Good job, Quinn."

"Thank you," Quinn said, searching for the right thing to say in this situation. She closed her mouth instead.

Phillip gestured to her. "Come on out with me, and let's check in with Velma on the system parameters to make sure everything went as planned. It shouldn't take too long."

Quinn placed the headgear on the rack and slid off the exam table to follow Phillip from the room. She tried to keep her expression neutral. She figured she'd still be under the control spell.

In the outer control room, Velma sat in her chair behind the bank of computers and screens, a puzzled frown plastered across her face.

Phillip glanced at her and laughed. "What's wrong? Did you forget to save the program files or something?"

"It's nothing like that. I just don't see anything on Quinn's vitals and system stats showing she got the kill, even though we got word she did."

Phillip shook his head. "That's impossible, I know what Barry sent in his text." Phillip turned back to Quinn. "You said you got the target. Did one of the others kill your target, like before?"

Quinn shook her head. "No, nothing like that. I killed her. She ran, and I chased her for a long time until we ran through an industrial park. We were fighting right by the docks. I tackled her, and she wrestled with me. She was stronger than I thought she would be, so I kicked her off me. I got up and reached for my Bowie to finish her off, but before I could do anything, she lost her balance and fell off the pier into the water. She splashed some, but by the time I got to the edge, she was slipping under. She must've been injured or something and just drowned."

Phil glanced at Velma.

She shrugged and looked back at her bank of screens. She tapped a few keys on the keyboard and stared at the results. "That makes sense. If she'd registered the kill, it would show up here. The target shows as dead according to my information. It's just not giving her the kill."

Phillip shook his head, scowling. "So it's likely that her kill wasn't official?"

"That's what it looks like, even if it's not fair," Velma said.

"It's not about fair or not fair." Phillip stopped as if about to say something else. He paused and then said, "At least all the targets are dead. That's another potential group of adversaries out of the way. In the meantime, we'll have to figure out another mission quickly so she can catch up with the others."

Quinn worked at keeping her facial expression blank as she stood there. She wasn't sure how much of the charm and control spell would still be in effect after her time in the VR system.

Phillip glanced at Quinn's face. She tried not to return his stare and kept looking past him at the wall. "Dammit, she's still caught under that spell she had when she got here. That Audrey has no finesse. As usual, she's poured it on too thick.

He raised his arms, sketching invisible shapes in the air inches from Quinn's face. At the same time, he muttered something in that same strange language Quinn didn't understand.

Beneath her bodysuit, a flare of sharp cold from the

amulet almost made her bring up her hand to rub it. She caught herself with her arm raised halfway and shifted her hand to rub the side of her head.

Quinn squeezed her eyes shut for a second and then opened them, locking eyes with Phillip. "I feel strange. What did you do?"

Phillip smiled and shook his head. "Nothing, really. It's just a little post-hypnotic suggestion trick that seems to help with the transition from the VR system. You should be fine now."

Quinn smiled at him. "Thanks. How did I do?"

"You did satisfactorily, but we will need to put you back in again tomorrow in order to get you your first registered kill. The target today didn't count, even though you were responsible for chasing her into the water. Next time, you need to use your knife on the target and do it right."

Quinn attempted to look disappointed, letting her shoulders sag while she frowned. She hoped that would be enough.

"Go get changed. We'll see what's going to happen next. I don't know if they're planning another assembly since you all have already been through the process once. Come back here after you've changed. Velma and I will have an idea of what time we'll be ready for another session tomorrow."

Quinn nodded and turned toward the door. Once in the hall, she headed back to the locker room. She'd once again avoided killing, but she knew she wouldn't be as lucky a third time. She had to get out of here with Taylor tonight. Then she could contact Clark and get him to help her do what was needed to save Taylor's soul, or whatever had been done to her in the VR system.

When she entered the locker room, the other female candidates were already there. Taylor was already almost completely dressed in her street clothes.

She smiled at Quinn as her friend walked over to the lockers. "I'm so excited you got your first kill in the system, Quinn. Didn't it give you a rush?"

Quinn nodded. "Um, yeah, I guess so. Pretty cool."

"Wait until you get your second. It's even stronger. I felt like my skin was vibrating all over when my target died under my blade today. I still sort of feel it now."

Taylor held an arm out to show her forearm covered in goosebumps. She rubbed the arm with her other hand as she dropped it back down to her side.

Quinn listened as Taylor described every detail of her kill, one of the women who'd been with Miranda in the protection circle.

She hurried to dress, half-listening as a candidate named Cindy chimed in to describe her second kill once Taylor was finished.

The other two women fell into comparing different aspects of their kills, marveling at the realism they'd experienced.

Quinn wanted to shout at them. She wanted to tell them it was real, and they'd just killed real people with families and friends and others who would miss them now that they were gone.

Instead, she pulled on her sneakers. She had to get out of here and take Taylor with her. An ominous feeling of dread had crept into her mind, as if something terrible was about to happen.

As Quinn was tying her shoelaces, the system monitor named Audrey came in the locker room again. She pointed at Taylor and Cindy. "You two, come with me. You both did a great job getting your second kills today. We want to reward you."

Taylor beamed with pride, as did the short redhead named Cindy. Both girls shut their lockers and followed Audrey out of the room.

Quinn called after Audrey. "Hey, wait up. I want to be there when you go up on the stage."

Audrey glared at Quinn. "This is a private ceremony for a select few of the best candidates. There seems to be some discrepancy surrounding your kill today. My colleagues are investigating what happened. I'd suggest you focus on whether you'll still have a job here this time tomorrow."

Taylor gave Quinn a half-smile and shrugged before following Audrey and Cindy out of the room.

Quinn called after them, "I'll wait for you in the parking lot, Taylor."

Audrey held the door for the two candidates she'd summoned. "Go home, Miss Faust. We will see to getting Taylor back home this evening if she so desires."

The woman let the door swing closed. Quinn glanced around and realized all the other candidates had left while she was dressing. She stood alone in front of her locker as she struggled with what to do next.

Quinn suspected what was going to happen to her friend and the other girl. If she was right about their fate, she needed to figure out a way to help Taylor before it was too late. Once her friend was possessed or whatever they planned on doing to her, Quinn didn't think it would be easy to get her to leave again.

She stuffed the rest of her clothes into her gym bag before shutting it and looping the strap over her shoulder. She had to hurry if she was going to catch up and figure out where Taylor was being taken.

Quinn darted out into the hallway. Looking both ways, she turned right in time to spot Taylor and Cindy turning the corner at the far end of the hall, heading toward the stairwell that led to the basement level.

Cursing, Quinn ran through the options in her mind. She was sure they were being taken downstairs. Audrey was going to cast a spell on them so they could be stripped naked and covered with runes in preparation for some demonic ceremony.

Quinn started after them when Phillip's voice sounded from behind her.

"Quinn, where are you going? You were supposed to come back to meet with Velma and me about additional mission options tomorrow."

Quinn turned and smiled at Phillip, trying to come up with a reason to chase her friend.

He stalked up the hallway in her direction. "I asked you where you were going?"

"I wanted to ask Taylor something. She and Cindy were headed off to an awards meeting or something like that."

Phillip glanced past Quinn down the corridor and shifted his gaze back to her. "Don't worry about her. You can catch up with her later if she's available. You've got other things to worry about. Come with me."

Quinn followed her system monitor. She spared a quick look over her shoulder at the empty hallway, trying to figure out some excuse not to go with Phillip.

Unable to come up with anything, Quinn resigned herself to going with him and getting through this meeting as quickly as possible. Then she could try to track Taylor down.

CHAPTER FIFTEEN

The meeting with Phillip and Velma wasn't long, lasting only about ten minutes while they tried to find another target scenario on short notice. Quinn knew that probably meant they were scrambling to find another victim for her to hunt down and kill.

The whole process disgusted her, but she waited patiently while Velma scanned a list on one of her screens until a likely scenario came up.

Velma pointed at the screen. "I found one. I can probably program a suitable scenario interface by late tomorrow afternoon. Quinn, can you be back here at four tomorrow?"

"Sure," Quinn lied. She had no intention of ever coming back to this place once she got herself and Taylor out of here.

Phillip nodded. "Good, we'll see you then. None of the others will be here. It'll just be you since this is a custom test session. Don't be late."

"I won't. Can I go now? I want to catch up with Taylor."

Phillip shook his head and said, "You can go, but Taylor is in a private meeting right now and won't be available for a while. Go home. Her monitors will make sure she makes it back safe and sound once things are finished here. Don't wait up. She might be here a while."

Quinn resisted the urge to shout her suspicions at the man. Instead, she nodded and said, "Sounds good. I'll see you both back here tomorrow."

She left them inside the control room, letting the door close behind her as she leaned against the wall outside. Quinn let out a long, slow breath, calming herself. She had to think carefully to work out a plan of some sort to get Taylor out of this mess.

Going through her options, Quinn started down the hall, heading through the doors to the long hallway that lead both to the front lobby and back to the gym and stairwell down to the lower level.

After making sure no one was in sight, Quinn turned right and started toward the gym and stairwell. When she reached the far end where the gym was located, she glanced over her shoulder for one last check.

Still in the clear, she turned the corner and moved into the stairwell. She waited to see if anyone followed her by watching through the small window in the stairwell door.

Voices drifted up from below. Quinn moved to the edge of the landing and peeked over the rail to the lower level.

She didn't see anyone, and the voices started to fade as if they were moving away.

Her heart thumping inside her chest, Quinn moved as silently as possible down the steps. Reaching the basement level, Quinn went to the door and peered through the window. Taylor and Cindy stood in the hallway on the other side, along with Fergus. The three of them followed Audrey and another monitor down the hall toward the room with the metal tables at the far end.

Quinn leaned back and struggled to come up with a plan. She didn't know how she could possibly follow them without being seen. Then she remembered what Clark had told her about her amulet giving her additional abilities.

If she could use that hiding ability Clark had described to her, she might be able to get close enough to find a way to free Taylor before it was too late.

Quinn reached inside her shirt, pulling out the amulet and grasping it tightly in one hand. She stared into the shadows at the base of the stairs while she thought about being hidden, trying to concentrate on making herself unseen. She didn't really expect it to work, but she had to try something.

Whispering the word "mist," Quinn backed into a shadow by the doorway at the bottom of the steps.

To her surprise, the amulet grew cold in her grasp and her vision became cloudy, as if she were seeing through fog.

She glanced at her hand and realized the fog covered only her body. When she focused on the stairs or the door, her vision cleared, although a hazy blur lingered around the edges.

Quinn marveled at the effect but wasn't sure she'd achieved what she wanted. Would it work?

There was only one way to find out. Quinn took a deep breath and pulled open the door. She stepped into the basement passage at the same instant a man entered the far end of the hall and started in her direction. He wore the strange black robes with the red lining she'd found in one of the rooms down here earlier. He gave no indication he saw her when she stepped into view.

As he approached her end of the hall, Quinn moved to the left-hand side, keeping her back pressed against the wall. He passed her without noticing her and stopped at one of the locked doors near the stairwell entrance. After pulling a keycard from his pocket, he used it on the panel next to the door, and it clicked open. He went inside.

Quinn glanced past him as he entered and saw a rack filled with an assortment of bladed weapons. She even saw a Bowie knife similar to the one she carried inside the VR system.

Moving closer to the open door, Quinn waited until the man came out again. He walked past her, back down the hallway. She spotted a dagger with a thin, curved blade in his hand before he tucked it under his cloak.

Quinn dodged past him as he went by, catching the door before it closed all the way. She slipped inside the room and let the door shut behind her.

Turning to scan the racks of weapons, Quinn pulled down the Bowie knife she'd seen from the hallway. Its polished blade reflected her image as she stared at it.

The grip fit in her hand as naturally as the one inside the VR system. She stared at it while twisting it to catch the light from overhead. Did she really need this?

Considering the dagger the man just left with, as well as the fact that they had a room like this, Quinn decided she did. She also noted several open slots on the weapons rack.

It appeared others might be carrying blades as well. It would be better if she was armed.

The blade's razor-sharp edge meant she couldn't just shove it in the waistband of her jeans. On the rear wall were assorted sheaths and belts, both leather and tactical webbing.

Quinn found a black leather sheath matching the Bowie and threaded a black canvas web belt through it. She settled the belt around her waist so the Bowie hung on her left side, angled to the front so she could reach across and draw it with her right hand.

She practiced drawing it a few times. It felt strangely natural to her, as if she'd done it before in real life and not just inside a VR game. She squeezed the bowie's hilt, testing the feel of the pebbled leather under her fingers. Nodding, she sheathed it as a big grin spread across her face.

Armed now, Quinn opened the door a crack to make sure no one was in the corridor before stepping back outside. The hazy film around her visual field told her the hunter amulet's magic was still in play.

Quinn passed the short hallway with the elevator entrance and finally reached the end of the hallway. She expected to see the man with the curved dagger in there, and he was. But he wasn't alone.

Inside the room with the metal tables, the man with the dagger stood next to Audrey. Both wore the black robes. The two of them had their hands and arms raised beside one of the tables. They chanted in deep tones while sketching invisible symbols and shapes in the air with their forefingers.

Quinn stifled a gasp as she caught a view of the naked form on the table when Audrey and the man shifted their positions to stand at the head and foot of the table.

It was Taylor. She lay there, her body as rigid as a board, with her arms at her sides and her eyes open, staring at the ceiling. She didn't blink or shift her gaze as the two moved around her working their magic.

The two continued chanting for a few seconds, then lowered their arms and stared down at Taylor.

Quinn glanced at the other tables. Each was occupied, with Cindy on the one closest to Taylor. Quinn spotted two other candidates, also naked on the final two tables. One of them was Fergus. All seemed to be in the same comatose state as Taylor.

The man reached into his robe and pulled out a small jar with a cork stopper and a thin-handled black stick.

No, not a stick. It was a narrow paintbrush.

He walked over to Cindy and uncorked the glass jar, then took the curved dagger from beneath his robe. Lifting Cindy's hand, he cut an inch-long gash in her palm and held the dripping blood over the top of the open jar.

After several dozen drops of fresh blood had made their way into the bottle, he put her hand down at her side and stirred at the jar with the paintbrush. He then began painting black runes and geometric shapes on Cindy's bare skin like the ones she'd seen on the earlier candidates in this room.

Across from him, Audrey had produced a similar bottle and brush and repeated the process on Taylor. They both moved quickly, with the efficiency that denoted long prac-tice at this process.

Quinn stood outside, watching them through the window in the door. As she did, a red flash at the edge of her vision caught her eye.

She twisted her head to see what it was, expecting an attack or something. When she saw nothing behind her, Quinn tried to understand she had seen. It took her a few seconds to notice it came from the masking spell she had in place. The red flashed with increasing frequency and intensity.

Realization dawned on her. The amulet's magic was fading or getting ready to end. Quinn glanced around; she needed to find a place to hide and quickly.

She pulled open the door closest to her, slipping inside what turned out to be an empty closet.

Quinn waited to see if anyone had seen the door open and close. She stood by the door, her hand touching the hilt of the sheathed Bowie, ready to draw it and defend herself.

While she listened for footsteps, the haze flashed red one last time and disappeared. Quinn touched the amulet with her right hand, finding that it was no longer cold.

Quinn filed that piece of information. Her amulet had limitations. It looked like this particular skill only lasted about twenty minutes at a time. It was probably intended to cover a hunter's escape or approach.

Keeping this in mind, Quinn wondered how long the amulet needed to recharge before she could activate the skill again. She tried to turn it on once more, but nothing happened. The amulet didn't change temperature, and she didn't see the hazy covering over her body either.

Quinn realized she was stuck in this room for a little

while, so she settled in to wait until the coast was clear. She worried about Taylor and what might happen to her if they managed to finish the prep for whatever demonic rite they had planned. She had to get her friend free.

Opening the door a crack, she could just see the edge of the window into the nearby room. Every now and then for the next half-hour, a figure would pass it.

Eventually, someone came to the door of the other room and pulled it open. Quinn let the closet door close as she listened.

"It looks like you have this in hand," Audrey said. "I'm heading back upstairs. I'll see you later this evening at the ceremony. This should be a good batch for our purposes."

"Will the gem be up to transforming so many in one batch?" a male voice asked.

"Myles seems to think so. If not, they'll keep until the energy recharges. We have enough acolytes in attendance to provide the blood needed to complete the charging process."

"True. Very well, I'll transport the last one down to the caverns. See you at the rites later."

The clack of Audrey's heels on the floor passed the room where Quinn hid and disappeared into the distance.

Quinn decided her best option was to attempt to over-power the robed man before he took the final comatose candidate down to the caverns, wherever that was.

She was about to make her move when the chime sounded from the elevator down the hall. Quinn tamped down her frustration and closed the door again, leaving it open just enough to see a thin sliver of the hallway outside.

A pair of black-robed figures passed, heading toward

the preparation room. Quinn picked up the murmur of voices as they entered the room that had held her friend, but she couldn't make out what they said.

Taking a chance, she stuck her head out far enough to see into the prep room. She was just in time to see all three men moving through the door on the opposite side of the room. Each wheeled a table with a naked figure on it down a hall on the other side and then out of sight. The door closed behind them.

Since the other door in the preparation room opened with a keycard, Quinn needed another plan to get Taylor out now.

Even if she made it through the locked door, she'd never be able to take on all three of them without raising an alarm of some sort. Plus, there was no guarantee she'd be able to remove the spell on Taylor and the others.

She was in over her head. Quinn ducked back into the closet and took off the belt and sheathed Bowie, tucking them into her gym bag for later, then headed back to the stairwell. She moved fast to get out of sight before anyone else saw her.

Quinn decided to try to get out of the building to her Jeep. Once she'd left the property, she could contact Clark. Her only chance was to convince him to help her make the rescue.

CHAPTER SIXTEEN

Quinn returned to the main floor without encountering anyone. A few of the other candidates came out as well. They must have been working late on something with their monitors. There were three in all, two women and a guy. She wasn't sure of their names, so she just smiled and nodded at them as she joined them. They all headed for the parking lot.

Quinn made a beeline to her Jeep. She unlocked it and climbed in, taking a deep breath and letting it out slowly to calm herself. Every muscle in her body hummed with tension as if ready to spring into combat. She'd never felt like this before.

She needed to get out of here and gather her thoughts while she reached out to Clark for assistance. She didn't know how, but she had to convince him to help her get Taylor free.

Starting the Jeep, Quinn pulled out of her parking spot and drove toward the main gate. When she got there, there were several cars in line, waiting to leave. A pair of armed guards stood by the gate, talking to the driver of the lead vehicle beneath the overhead lamp by the guard shack.

They kept pointing back toward the main building and parking area. Quinn didn't like the look of it when one of the guards proceeded to walk up the line of cars, stopping to talk to each of the drivers.

She wound her window down and leaned out as the guard finally approached her Jeep. "Is the gate broken or something? I need to get home."

"You'll have to go back and park, miss. We have the premises on lockdown. I'm not sure what the issue is, but you'll need to return inside with the others and get permission from your direct supervisor before we can allow you to leave."

Quinn shook her head. "I am already late for something else. Isn't there some way you can let me slide? You can search my Jeep if you want. I swear I haven't stolen anything."

Quinn smiled, but the guard didn't return it. He lifted his right hand and rested it on the butt of his pistol in its holster.

"Miss, like I said, you'll have to go back and park. If you want to leave, you'll need your supervisor to call out here and give us specific permission. Until we hear from them, everyone stays put."

For a few seconds, Quinn considered trying to steer around the others and ram through the metal gate, but she wasn't sure she'd be able to break through. Plus, if she did that, she wouldn't be able to come back and help Taylor.

Hiding her disappointment behind another smile, Quinn shrugged. "Okay. you're just doing your job. I understand. I'll go get permission and be back in a few minutes."

Quinn looked over her shoulder as she backed the Jeep out of the driveway. She was able to turn around once the road widened, and she drove back to the main parking lot.

After parking in the nearly empty lot, this time much closer to the building, Quinn walked back into the building. As she crossed the lobby, she spotted Velma coming through the double doors leading into the VR test wing. "Quinn, I thought you'd already left."

"I got hung up because I forgot something in the locker room. Now I can't leave for some reason. What's going on? I thought we were done for the day."

Velma shook her head. "There's been some sort of security breach. Everyone needs to stay put until we figure out what happened."

"What sort of security breach? You mean, like someone hacked into the system?"

"I'm not going to share details with you. It's not something you need to worry about." Velma turned to address the other three candidates who'd been stopped at the gate with Quinn. "Come on back into the training wing. We are setting up places there for you to stay until we get this figured out."

Quinn started to follow Velma toward the hallway leading back to the testing area. "How long do you plan on keeping us here? The way you said that makes it sound like we'll be here overnight."

Velma glanced over her shoulder. "We've got cots laid out and food being prepared for you. You'll be comfortable enough. Besides, you're all getting paid overtime to stay and sleep here, so what do you care?"

Quinn followed Velma with the others. They turned down a hallway just past the locker rooms. Quinn was unfamiliar with this area and tried to see where they were going. Velma led them down the hall to an open room laid out like a small dining area with several tables and chairs.

Six folding cots had been rolled into the room and stood by the door. Velma turned to the group of candidates and said, "Move the tables and chairs out of the way so you have room to open the cots."

Quinn pointed to the cots. "There are six of them. Are we expecting two more people?"

Velma shook her head. "No. They weren't sure how many of you were still here. Just push them off to the side with the tables. Get settled in, and get some sleep. I don't think we'll get this sorted out before morning. We'll have someone come by with food for you."

The candidates started sliding the furniture to the side. Quinn helped a girl with bright orange hair stack the chairs to make more room for the cots.

Once they had the center of the room cleared, Quinn and the others unfolded four of the cots. Inside were a set of white sheets, a thin gray blanket, and a pillow.

She made her bed, unsure of what else to do in this situation. Velma stood nearby, watching Quinn and the others at work.

Once the cot was set up, Quinn sat down, trying to decide what she should do next. She decided to pull out her phone and reach out to Clark on the number she'd called earlier. Maybe he'd have ideas she could use to get out of here. She texted because she couldn't talk in front of everyone.

She'd tapped in the first few numbers of Clark's contact when Velma pointed to Quinn. "Put that away."

"I was just..."

"All of you, turn off your phones completely, not just silenced. Turn them off and put them away."

The other candidates did as they were asked without hesitation or complaint. Quinn realized this was a residual effect of the compulsion and control spells they used on the candidates. She had to play along or she'd get caught.

Velma's eyes narrowed as she stared at her.

Hiding a sigh, Quinn switched off her phone and dropped it into an outer pocket on her gym bag.

Velma left the room, flipping off the overhead lights as she did. She did leave the door ajar, so a little light filtered in from outside.

The others took the hint and began to settle in and get ready for bed. They were strangely complacent and didn't say much to each other as they got ready to sleep. They followed Velma's orders without resistance. Once again, she silently thanked her amulet for eventually breaking through her control spells while she was in VR earlier.

Stuck for the night, Quinn realized she was going to have to figure a way out of this herself. First on the list, she had to find a way to free Taylor from whatever they had in store for her in the area below.

Quinn didn't know what that might be, other than not liking the mention of a cavern, a ceremony, and bloodletting to recharge some magic gem. Part of Quinn still didn't believe in demons, but she'd seen magic at work now, so she had to assume demons were real, too.

As the other candidates laid down and settled in to sleep, Quinn did the same. It wouldn't do for her to not appear compliant with orders if Velma came back.

She stared at the ceiling for a few seconds, then closed her eyes.

Quinn's mind raced as she tried to figure out some way to get out of here. If only she could get away and call Clark.

CHAPTER SEVENTEEN

Clark glanced at his watch for what seemed like the tenth time in as many minutes.

"She'll call," Miranda said. "Don't worry."

Clark shook his head as he paced around the small apartment where he and Miranda sat waiting. "It's been hours since we got back. She should've returned and been able to leave by now."

"You still haven't explained to me exactly how she showed up like she did and then returned to that corporate complex north of the city so quickly."

Clark shrugged. "I'm not sure I understand it either. My best guess is it's probably a hybrid mixture of technology and magic that have somehow been combined to defeat standard protection magic. That was how they got past your wards and found you. You hadn't warded against technology, just magical detection. I seem to remember several of the clans' best mages were working on something similar in theory before the purge. These bastards must've had a breakthrough to transport the candidates inside this virtual reality game they've created. If the little information Quinn gave me was true, the system can send them directly to targets they're tracking."

Miranda nodded. She glanced down and tapped the phone in her hand, checking for messages.

Clark pointed to the phone. "Any word?"

Miranda looked up with a pained expression on her face. She had tears welling in her eyes. "I still haven't heard from them. They must be dead, or they would've checked in by now."

Clark shook his head. He didn't want to say anything yet, but he'd had several text reports from his police contacts. They reported unexplained murders in the city around that area. He had no confirmation that it was her people, so he kept it to himself.

He forced a smile. "Let's continue to hope for the best. You got away. Maybe some of them got away safely, too."

"I only escaped because the hunter chasing me changed her mind. This girl, Quinn…who is she to you? What's the connection?" Miranda asked.

Clark shrugged. "I'm not really sure. She might be related to me, a distant cousin or possibly closer. One thing I'm sure of—she's definitely the child of a hunter family. At least one of her parents was from a hunter clan."

"I thought it was rare for your people to marry outside the community."

"It was, but it was not unheard of. At the end, just before the purges started, things started relaxing more and more as the elders tried to bring fresh blood into the clans to rejuvenate our powers to what they used to be. That might be how Quinn's parents escaped the purge, at least initially. They may not have been living close to the others in the community. Maybe they lived with the mundane side of their family."

"One thing is for sure, Clark. When she does get back in touch with you, you have to get her out of that place, whatever it takes. The magic needed to do what you think they're doing has to be significant. My coven had detected a surge of netherworld power recently. It was sporadic, but when we picked up on it, it displayed as a huge spike all at once. Based on what you've told me and what we discovered before they attacked us, there's no way an untrained girl with no understanding of the power she has at her disposal can hold her own in there."

"That's what I'm afraid of. I didn't want her going back, but given that she somehow found you in time to save you, I guess that was a good thing. Of course, now she needs to get herself out."

"Do you know where the office complex is?"

"She told me the name of the company. I looked it up and did some research, so I know the address. I can't tell who owns it, though. The organization is hidden under several shell companies. There's no way to nail down exactly who's in charge. That leads me to believe it is probably owned by our adversaries."

Miranda stood. "Perhaps we should think about going up there and checking the place out for ourselves, then. We could at least drive by and see if I can detect anything about what's going on inside. There's no way they can completely shield that much power."

"That's what I've been thinking. I keep hoping Quinn will call and tell me she's out. She has the number of a friend of mine. They've forwarded that line directly to me, so I'll get the call. I'm afraid she's pigheaded enough to stay if she can't convince her friend to leave before it's too late."

"She not only seems to have been born a hunter, but she also carries the values of one. You'd never leave a friend behind either, am I right?"

Clark shot her a glance, wondering if she knew something about his past. Realizing it was a harmless comment, he said, "So it would seem. None of that will help her if she gets into a difficult situation, though. She has no training or knowledge of what her inherent abilities are. There's so much she should have learned growing up. I gave her clues to that ability to hide in the shadow, but it won't save her by itself."

"We all come into our skills and strengths in due time. When I first discovered I was a witch, I was young. I hid my ability from those around me because I was embarrassed. I learned to do many things on my own before I received anything approaching formal training. Perhaps she is stronger and more capable than you know."

"I hope so. There is so much I could teach her, given a few weeks to do it."

"Like what?"

"The abilities are inherent in her genes, but without proper training, she can't possibly make the most of them. The amulet will help her activate some things, but others require intense training and meditation to unlock. My limited understanding from those who used to study the science behind such things is to think of it as a sort of recessive gene that needs to be switched on. That is done in different ways, depending on the skill and the individual. Some are activated magically, and others through specific situations and training. That is what I plan to do once she gets out of there. It won't take me long to understand the scope of her potential."

"Perhaps the situation she's in now will do that for her."

Clarks considered, then picked up his keys from the table. "Let's go. We'll swing by VirSync like you suggested. I don't want to leave you here unattended and unprotected. We won't get too close, but at least we can drive by and see what the place looks like."

Miranda nodded and picked up her purse and slung the bag's long strap over her head and across her chest so it hung at her waist.

From its size, Clark guessed it held components for some of her spells. Maybe she'd have something to offer to get Quinn out if she came along.

He went to the apartment door, checked the hallway outside for any danger, and then held it for Miranda. "After you."

Miranda nodded as she passed him. Clark fell in behind her as they headed down the steps to the street.

It took them almost a half-hour to reach the industrial park north of the city where VirSync was located. As they drove past it, Clark noticed the tall stone and iron fence surrounding the building and grounds.

That and the gated entry would serve to keep most intruders out. It would probably keep prisoners inside as well.

Clark glanced at Miranda. When they'd gotten close, she'd pulled several items out of her bag. She now held a crystal suspended from a silver chain in front of her face as they drove, and gazed into its interior intensely.

"Anything yet?"

Miranda shook her head, not taking her eyes of the crystal. "I don't see anything inherently evil. There are standard magical wards in place, though. This has to be the right place. What ordinary company would even know to use magic like that? I still don't see any trace of demonic intrusion."

Clark agreed with her first point. No one used magic, aside from the few free witch covens and the occasional rogue hunter like Clark. If they used magic to ward their property, they had to be working with demonic forces seeking a foothold in the world.

He looked at the road as he asked, "The question I have is how they arrived at the method to combine technology and magic the way they have?"

"I'm not sure, but there have been reports that members of the human scientific community detected the existence of magical power sources like ley lines and such. Perhaps the scientists working here used that knowledge to spring-board their hybrid of the two, and are using it to protect the facility as well as to fuel their hunting parties."

Clark glanced at the wall as they drove around the complex of buildings. "Well, we know she's in there. I tagged her Jeep with a tracking spell the other night. As we drove past the main gates, I could tell it's parked some-where inside. I don't detect anything of a netherworld nature, do you? If what I think is happening is true, why isn't there a taste of vile magic here?"

Miranda shook her head. "There's none I can detect.

That doesn't mean it isn't there. There are ways to conceal such things from those on the side of the light, just as we have ways to conceal things from them. Those who are tuned to one side or the other give up the ability to see the full spectrum of magic."

Clark didn't like her answer, so he continued driving around the perimeter of the property.

While tracing the magical wards as they circled the area, Miranda looked for a break in the defenses. She found nothing promising.

Clark spotted no easy way past the wall, other than the gated entrance. The barrier could be scaled, but with the combination of magical wards and technological security systems, it wouldn't be easy.

After passing the main entrance for the second time, Clark stopped in the parking lot of a nearby storage facility. They could still see the stone and concrete wall surrounding VirSync on the opposite side of the road.

It was late, and the storage center employees had all left for the day. He parked at the far end of the lot, away from the nearest overhead light, and turned off the engine.

Pulling his phone from his pocket, he checked it for messages once again, then set it on the dashboard in front of him while he checked his watch. It was ten o'clock, and still no word.

"If we don't hear from her soon, I think I need to find a way to get in there and go after her."

Miranda laid a hand on his forearm. "You have no idea what they have in there. At the very least, there are numerous spell-casters. Something as major as teleporting that many individuals even the short distance to the center of the city would require a coven of enormous size, twenty or more individuals."

"What else can I do? She's the first hunter survivor I've found in over a decade. Perhaps there are others. Without realizing it, she might even know about some from being in the city's foster system. It's possible other members of the local clan hid their children as well."

Miranda offer him a gentle smile. "Let's wait and see if we hear from her. We are ready and close by if she needs us and reaches out. That is probably the best thing we can do for now."

Clark ground his teeth. The frustration was nearly too much for him. He'd been doing what he could to protect people from attack in the area while remaining hidden. It never occurred to him there would be other hunter survivors besides the very few he knew of across the country. The fact that there might be children who grew up without knowledge of their legacy bothered him. He should have known they'd be out there or at least suspected it.

He had to get Quinn out of there and set things right.

Clark clenched his fists on the steering wheel, working to control his frustration as he considered the scarcity of options.

"I don't like waiting, but I agree with you. I don't think there's anything else we can do. We'll wait for her to call. It's a big building, and several others nearby are attached to it. I have no idea where she is inside, so it would be a failed mission from the beginning to just charge in there."

Miranda nodded and returned her gaze to the crystal

suspended from her raised hand while she muttered a new spell at it.

When she finished, Clark asked, "What did you just do?"

"I masked the vehicle so no suspicious security guards or passing police officers will notice us. We should be good here for the rest of the night. I also sent out a query via a nearby ley line to try to understand where they might be drawing their power from. If they are using the type of magic you suspect, there should be some way to register the power draw now that we know where they are."

Clark nodded. It wasn't much, but it would have to do for now. If Miranda was able to localize where the central power usage area was inside the building, he'd have a better idea of where to go if he decided to head inside after Quinn.

Until then, he'd have to be satisfied with waiting for her to contact him.

CHAPTER EIGHTEEN

Q uinn lay on her cot after Velma left them in the dark silence of their improvised dormitory. The others dozed for about twenty minutes, until Velma came back with Phillip to help.

They opened the door, pushing a cart into the room. It had a box on top filled with sandwiches and water bottles.

The candidates dove in, eating their fill, which amounted to several sandwiches each.

When all were finished, Phillip told them to lie down. "Someone will be back tomorrow with something for breakfast. Until then, get some sleep. We'll see you in the morning."

Quinn was midway through her third sandwich when the order to go to sleep came. She was strangely famished, feeling as if she hadn't eaten in more than a day, even though she'd had a hearty breakfast that morning and a decent lunch before coming to work.

Phillip's voice had the sound of command, and judging from the way the others responded, the control spell made them follow the order to the letter. Quinn quickly tucked a fourth sandwich under the blanket with a full water bottle as she lay down, too.

The two VirSync managers left, shutting off the light and closing the door all the way this time and plunging the room into total darkness.

Quinn laid still, waiting until she was sure the others were fully asleep. When she couldn't wait any longer, she opened her eyes and looked around, trying to peer through the darkness at the others. She had to be sure they were asleep.

Judging by the soft sounds of breathing, including one who was snoring, all of the other candidates had fallen asleep. Having full stomachs had helped, she was sure.

Strangely, as she laid in the dark an hour later, hunger pangs struck her again. Quinn dug under the blanket and pulled out the remains of the sandwich she'd been eating earlier. She wolfed it down, along with the fourth sandwich she'd grabbed, following them with the bottle of water she'd hidden.

As she finished her snack, Quinn wondered if the strange hunger was tied to her use of the amulet's magic earlier. Did its use gain power from her? Maybe that was why the masking spell had eventually failed—her energy had become depleted.

Quinn thought about it some more as she stood and reached out in the dark. She was still a little hungry, and she was pretty sure Velma had left the cart over by the door. There were some additional sandwiches in there, along with more water bottles.

She stumbled into something that banged painfully

against her shin, leaving her cursing under her breath. "Dammit, I need to see!"

A brief flash of chill against her chest caught her by surprise, but not as much as the sudden change in what she could see in the pitch-black room. The room was clearly lit now. It looked strange in the new light flooding her eyes—everything had a blueish hue, with all other colors muted to blue-gray and black.

Quinn smiled as she realized what she'd done. Not only could she hide herself with her magic, but she could also see in the dark. Quinn wondered what other hidden abilities she had.

She wanted to talk to Clark. Maybe he could tell her over the phone what other magic she could use to rescue Taylor.

Quinn crossed the room, dodging obstacles with ease now that she could see. She grabbed two more sandwiches, unwrapped one, and took a huge bite. She also cracked open a water bottle to wash it down. She finished both sandwiches in record time.

Quinn patted her full stomach. She felt much better now. Her energy seemed to be back to normal.

Testing her premise about how she fueled her newfound abilities, Quinn focused on the shadows around her and said "mist" as she concentrated. Once again, the haziness returned to the edges of her vision.

Quinn pumped her fist. She could go down and get Taylor now. She let go of the masking spell, letting it fade until she needed it, and returned to her cot to retrieve her gym bag.

A few seconds later, she'd pulled out her new Bowie

knife in its sheath. Quinn tightened the web belt around her waist and settled the weapon in place at her hip.

Next, she slung the strap of her gym bag over her shoulder and returned to the door. On the way out, she grabbed the last two water bottles and the remaining sandwich, dropping them in the gym bag.

Quinn zipped up the bag, slid it around to rest at the small of her back, and pulled the door open a crack. She stopped just in time to hear voices coming her way.

Quinn froze, hoping they didn't notice the door was ajar.

"The stone has recharged?" Myles Hickman said.

"Yes, my lord. It has been immersed in the blood given by the acolytes for a full twelve hours. It should contain enough power now to enable the transference for two or three of the candidates."

Myles sounded angry when he replied, "I do not understand why we cannot do more. We've been able to pull across four or five in the past with ease."

"We have been unable to ascertain why, my lord. There appears to be something in the vicinity that resists the energy draw the jewel uses."

"I don't like it when you tell me something like that without an answer as to how you're going to fix it, Jenkins. Figure out what's blocking the energy draw and get rid of it. Do you think perhaps there is a spy within the company? A rival witch or sorcerer?"

"I am not entirely sure…"

Quinn couldn't hear the rest. They'd moved too far down the corridor.

It was enough information to know they planned on

using some sort of magical gem or jewel for a ceremony with the candidates they'd prepared. That included Taylor.

Quinn needed to find a way to stop them before it was too late.

She waited for a count of ten, then pulled open the door, listening carefully before sticking her head out into the hallway.

It was clear. No one in sight.

She closed the door behind her and headed down the hall toward the main corridor that led past the locker rooms.

Only half of the lights in the building were currently on, probably an energy-saving feature used during night-time hours. She wasn't complaining since it helped her keep out of sight easier and dart into doorways before she was seen.

She didn't want to draw on her power right away since that might draw down her energy reserves. Quinn wasn't hungry after those last two sandwiches, but she didn't know how long that situation would hold. The last time, the spell had lasted for about twenty minutes, but that was after she'd gone on the hunt and everything.

Quinn decided to save using it for when she really needed it. She opted instead to move as silently as she could down the hall to the stairwell.

Checking to make sure no one was using the stairs, Quinn started down to the lower level.

When she reached the basement and approached the door, she heard voices on the other side. Pulling open the door just far enough to peer through it, she spotted three robed figures coming out from the room where she'd found the black robes earlier.

The trio continued down the passage away from her toward the room that had held Taylor and the others. Two of them pulled up the broad-hooded cowls attached to the cloaks so their heads were covered.

It gave her an idea.

Quinn concentrated and muttered, "Mist."

As soon as the spell hid her, she darted across the hall and caught the door to the robing room just in time to stop it from closing all the way.

Stepping inside, Quinn glanced at the rack that held the robes. Most of them were gone. There'd been twenty or thirty robes when she'd checked earlier. Whatever ceremony they had planned was probably beginning soon.

Quinn grabbed a robe from the rack and pulled it around her, slipping her hands into the sleeves and buttoning it up the front. It hung down to her ankles, hiding her blue jeans. If she walked slowly, they probably wouldn't see her sneakers. She pulled the hood up and over her head, hoping the shadows inside it would conceal her face from anyone who looked her way.

Taking a deep breath, Quinn let the hiding spell drop and stepped back out into the hallway to test her disguise.

There was no one there. The trio who'd been walking toward the far end was nowhere in sight.

Quinn started down the hall in a slow, steady walk, containing her desire to race to where they were keeping Taylor. A single robed individual remained in the room with the last table. Quinn's heart sank when she saw Taylor had already been taken. The remaining table held the guy she didn't know from the earlier trip down here. Taylor, and Cindy, and Fergus weren't anywhere in sight.

She fought down panic as she tried to figure out a way to get past the last robed figure.

The other robed person, a man with thinning gray hair she'd never seen before, turned and saw her through the window.

He pointed at her.

Quinn fought down the urge to run just in time to hear him say, "You, there. Help me pull this one down to wait in the chamber below. He must be anointed before going into the transference ceremony."

Swallowing hard, Quinn nodded, keeping her head down so the folds of the hood around her head partially hid her face as she answered. She pulled open the door and entered the room, moving to the table to stand by comatose guy's feet.

The man used his foot to unlock the table's wheels at his end. Quinn looked down and found the mechanism to do the same on her side.

The man nodded and pulled the table while Quinn pushed from her end. Together, they rolled the table toward the far door.

As the man approached the door, he pulled a standard VirSync photo badge and swiped it to open the door. That was good. She would have had trouble getting past the locked door without this guy's help.

He pushed the door open with his back as he pulled the wheeled table after him. Once Quinn got far enough to catch the door and to hold it open from her end, the guy turned around and walked facing forward as he steered the table along a narrow passage until they reached a sort of open freight elevator. It was like ones she'd seen at construction sites, with cage doors that moved up and down rather than a solid metal door.

Quinn stopped by the elevator. The open shaft disappeared into darkness below.

She stood still and waited for the elevator to come back up, having decided to be silent and just follow along at this point. Hopefully, her companion wouldn't try to carry on a conversation with her.

Luckily for her, the guy fiddled with his phone, sending messages back and forth to someone while he waited for the elevator to come up to their level. That was good as far as she was concerned.

The elevator arrived, and the cage door slid up. Quinn and the silent man steered the table into the elevator car. Quinn noted there were only two buttons, Up and Dn.

The guy pressed the Dn button, and the elevator lurched into motion.

Quinn's anxiety level ratcheted up several levels on the way deep underground. The elevator trip lasted for more than a minute. The whole time, all she could think about was how much she wanted to find Taylor. A strange dread that she might already be too late filled her.

Her fears would soon be confirmed.

At the bottom, they rolled the table off the elevator into a passage lit by a series of bare bulbs at intervals along the ceiling.

The walls and floor of the tunnel were only partially finished by human construction. The floor had been smoothed enough to allow them to roll the table down the gently sloping tunnel with relative ease.

After passing through two open caves, they reached an opening to the right where a large room had been carved out of the rock.

A single table with Taylor's body on it waited in the room, and a robed individual stood next to it. He leaned over Taylor as he muttered something, sticking his thumb in a small jar he held and smearing an oily substance on her forehead and in the center of her chest between her breasts.

He repeated the muttering and reapplied the oil several times before looking up at Quinn and the other guy.

She caught the hint of a grin from inside the shadows of his hood as he asked, "Is that the last one?"

The man with Quinn said, "Yes, he's the final one. I heard we might not be able to do all four tonight. Is that true?"

"That is what the master fears. I hope he doesn't take his displeasure out on any of us. I didn't sign up for this duty to the overlords to end up one of the possessed."

"None of us did. Have they already started?"

The man with the small jar of oil nodded. "They took the other girl as soon as I got down here. A pair of our brethren came up fifteen minutes ago to retrieve the first of the males. They should be almost finished with both by now. If you two are going down, you can take this one with you so she can go next."

Quinn realized with horror they'd been talking about Cindy and Fergus going down to the ceremony already. Taylor was next in line.

She worked through her few options. There had to be a way to get out of this and free Taylor, too.

The man who had come with Quinn nodded, locked the front wheels of the table he and Quinn brought, and moved to the table holding Taylor. He stood at its head and pointed at Quinn. "You coming?"

Quinn nodded and fell in at the foot of Taylor's table. Before he started down the passage, he pulled up his hood, hiding his face. Then, with Quinn's help, he began rolling Taylor's table deeper into the tunnels.

She was glad the other one had raised his hood. It meant any others down the passage likely wore theirs up as well. That would make it much easier for her to blend in.

The passage soon began to slope downward again, and with each step, more fear built up deep in her chest. The tons of stone and earth above her, trapping her below the ground, contributed to more dread than she thought she could stand.

She feared what she'd find farther down the tunnel, and what it would mean for her friend.

CHAPTER NINETEEN

As Quinn and the robed man headed down the passage, she went through what she knew and her options. First, VirSync wasn't just a company working for evil wizards or whatever, the whole place was apparently a cover for a cult of demon worshipers.

Second, a lot of what she could do to rescue Taylor depended on how many people were at the ceremony, and if they left Taylor alone at any time. Quinn didn't relish the idea of fighting the cultists, especially if it came to killing someone, whether they were already damned or not. If it meant saving Taylor's life, she'd do what it took, though.

On the way down the tunnel, several people in robes passed them, coming from the other direction. She'd hoped maybe she and the man at the head of the table would be alone in the passage long enough for her to find an excuse to stop and then jump him.

They were never alone long enough to give her a chance to try. All she could do was press her lips together in silence and keep her head down to hide her face in the shadows of her cowl.

Chanting drifted up as they continued downward. With each step, the chants grew louder. The words were in a language she couldn't understand, but their harsh, guttural sound made the hair on her arms stand on end.

About a hundred feet farther down, the tunnel opened into a large cavern. Although the rough walls and ceiling had been shaped by natural processes, the central portion of the cavern's floor had been smoothed, forming a circular area in the middle of the chamber.

From the center of the circle rose a carved stone pedestal about three feet across. The top had been hollowed out to form a shallow basin in which burned a pile of coals.

At least twenty other robed figures clustered around the stone brazier. In front of the pedestal, resting on one of the steel tables, Fergus was laid out for everyone to see, covered from head to toe in painted black runes and shapes. They'd arranged the table with his head near the pedestal.

Next to Fergus, a figure wearing a robe similar to Quinn's stood. It wasn't identical. His was embroidered with gold and silver thread, forming ornate patterns on the chest, shoulders, and sleeves.

The figure held a glowing red gem in their right hand. The jewel had been cut to form a flattened disc about two inches across and an inch thick. The leader slowly passed the stone over Fergus's body from head to toe, then back up again.

This must be the Ruby Heart she'd heard mentioned earlier.

When the stone passed over Fergus's head or chest, it pulsed brighter. This caused the assembled cultists to chant louder for a few seconds. Everyone's eyes were on the gem.

Having neared the rest of the group, Quinn and the man pulling Taylor along stopped beside an empty table.

Quinn realized it must have held Cindy at one time. She was nowhere in sight, so Quinn scanned the crowd to try to find her. Had they killed or sacrificed her?

At first, Quinn didn't see her. Then Quinn spotted a short redhead wearing robes and standing amidst the others clustered around the burning brazier.

Her hood was not drawn up, and Quinn stifled a gasp as she caught a glimpse of Cindy's eyes. The other woman looked in Quinn's direction with eyes that were completely black. It was as if the pupil had been expanded, no whites visible.

Cindy's black eyes seemed to glare in Quinn's direction for a few seconds before she turned calmly back to the ceremony around Fergus.

For a moment, Quinn worried that Cindy, or whatever she was now, had recognized her. She let out a long, slow breath of relief when the possessed woman didn't raise the alarm.

The chanting rose in volume again, finally ending with a shout from the chief priest. When she heard his voice over the others, Quinn recognized it. The leader of the ceremony was Myles Hickman.

Myles held the glowing gem in the air over his head.

The stone pulsed again with a surge of crimson light. When the light within the stone was at its brightest, he lowered the gem to Fergus's forehead.

The comatose figure came to life with a spasm that ran from head to toe.

Myles removed the gem and stepped back as Fergus sat up. His head swiveled from side to side in slow motion as if he were taking a panoramic picture of the room.

When Fergus's face turned Quinn's way, his eyes contained black pools of darkness just like Cindy's.

Myles raised both arms over his head and offered a deep bow to Fergus. "Rise, brother from the nether planes. We welcome you to our world."

He straightened from his bow and gestured to one of the other cultists nearby. The hooded figure came forward holding a black robe. The cultist helped Fergus put on the robe, then stepped back to their place in the group.

Fergus surveyed the group with a toothy grin, then the former candidate turned back to face Myles. "It has been a long while since I have walked in any form on this world. You have done well to summon so many of us to join your ranks these last few weeks. You must hurry to bring more. There are others among my brethren awaiting transference."

He still sounded like Fergus, sort of.

Quinn wasn't sure what she'd expected. There were differences. His voice now had a timbre that caused her skin to crawl. It was like there was a second, deeper voice in the background when he spoke. The amulet on her chest had grown colder and colder throughout the process of his turning. Now it seemed to be cold enough to freeze the skin beneath it.

Despite how uncomfortable it was, Quinn didn't dare reach for it, for fear it might draw attention to her. She'd just have to bear the discomfort.

Myles nodded in response to Fergus's command. "Yes, of course. We have an additional candidate already prepared for one of your companions to join us." He raised his hand and gestured past the other cultists in Quinn's direction.

The man at the head of Taylor's table turned around and hissed at Quinn to get her attention. "Come along. We mustn't keep him waiting. Be quick about it."

Quinn gripped the foot of the table as they rolled Taylor into position. Two other cultists had moved the other table out of the way to make room.

Fergus went over to stand beside Cindy while Taylor's table was arranged.

Myles stepped forward and raised the gem over his head. It had dimmed quite a bit since its last use, but it still pulsed with a faint inner glow.

He glanced at both Quinn and the man who'd delivered the table. "Return to your places."

Quinn backed up, joining the ranks of those encircling the ceremony. She positioned herself so she stood behind two others, trying to remain as far away from the light coming off the burning brazier as possible while remaining in a position to see Taylor.

Myles began chanting, and he was quickly joined by the others. She moved her mouth, letting a dull drone come out, trying to mimic the others without saying any actual words.

Myles passed the stone up and down Taylor's rune-covered form.

The chill in Quinn's amulet intensified again as the strange magic in it activated its inherent protections. A thought popped into her head. Could the protection it offered her be extended to someone else?

Given that the spell was already in progress, Quinn had to do something before Taylor was possessed by whatever type of being had taken over the other candidates.

Quinn pressed the chill of the amulet's magic deeper into her chest with two fingers. Though the cold now seared her skin, Quinn didn't wince or let out a sound. She focused all the energy from her pain and every ounce of her will on the amulet, directing its energy at Taylor.

She had no idea if it was working but it was all she could think to do.

The chanting continued and Myles moved on with the ceremony, passing the pulsing gemstone over Taylor's body as he worked on whatever magic he tried to cast.

Even though it looked like the ceremony was progressing, Quinn refused to give up.

She squeezed the amulet tighter through the robe's fabric, digging it into the skin in the center of her chest until the silver edges cut into her. The cold's intensity had increased to the point that it felt like a hot poker was pressed against her.

Quinn accepted the pain of the extreme cold and channeled it, boring into Taylor with her eyes to try to send some of the energy from the protection amulet into her friend.

Myles raised his voice as he continued chanting.

That was when Quinn heard it.

His voice was different. It seemed strained or doubtful, or maybe both. Although she couldn't understand the language they used, Myles's words had taken on a desperate tone.

The magical gemstone also looked different now. When she'd arrived, it had steadily increased in intensity as it pulsed over Fergus. Now, though, it had dimmed.

Myles brought up his other hand and held the gem between both of them. His knuckles whitened as he applied pressure. He seemed to be trying to squeeze more power from it.

Quinn, through a haze of icy agony, realized whatever she was doing was working. She gathered her remaining will and pushed her amulet's magic at her friend with more intensity.

Quinn visualized pushing the pulsing red glow back into the depths of the gem so it couldn't work its magic. She'd never attempted anything like that before; it was sort of like trying to hold onto fine sand.

Myles snarled a curse and lowered the gem to his side, eliciting an alarmed shout from the assembled cultists. He lowered his cowl and wiped beads of sweat from his forehead with the back of his free hand.

The chanting around the circle petered out, and everyone fell silent.

Cindy, or the person who used to be Cindy, turned her

black eyes toward Myles. "What is wrong? Why do you not proceed?"

Myles shook his head, staring at the gemstone with a puzzled expression. "We have used the stone enough today. I thought there was enough energy remaining from yesterday to bring three of your comrades through. Unfortunately, it appears to be unable to do so."

"I do not care for idle excuses. If you begin the ceremony, you should finish it. Our masters will not be pleased."

A chorus of concerned murmurs spread through the robed figures surrounding the brazier.

Myles's expression changed from perplexed to alarmed, or perhaps even desperate at Cindy's last statement. "We will bring the remainder of your group through tomorrow. In the meantime, please come with me while my underlings recharge the stone so it will be ready tomorrow."

Cindy and Fergus nodded, fixing the VirSync CEO with their black eyes. They moved over to follow him as he walked through the cluster of cultists.

As he passed Quinn and the man who'd brought Taylor down, Myles said, "Place her back in the upper chamber with the other one. We will prepare them both for transference tomorrow."

The man nodded and bowed as Myles passed. "It will be as you say, my lord."

Quinn duplicated the bow, using it as an excuse to keep her face hidden from the high priest as he and the possessed candidates stalked by, heading back up the passageway.

As Quinn rose from her bow, she caught sight of the

gemstone, which sat on a brass plate resting on the coals in the center of the brazier. Lying next to it on the edge of the stone pedestal was a long iron knife. The black blade looked pitted and crudely fashioned.

The assembled cultists began to line up, blocking Quinn's view of both the brazier and the gem. Each went to the pedestal for a few seconds, then moved on, making room for the others in line behind them.

Quinn couldn't make out what they were doing, so she moved closer to stand next to the table where Taylor lay.

A tug at the table drew her attention back to the man at the other end.

He sneered at her. "Unless you want to sacrifice your blood to recharge that damned gem, I'd keep moving. We've been given another task by the high priest, but if the others see us here, they'll expect us to join them in the blood ritual."

Quinn nodded, resisting the urge to glance over her shoulder at the line of cultists. She pushed her end of the table, helping the man steer it back up the tunnel. They soon arrived at the side chamber, where the other table with the final male candidate sat.

She helped situate Taylor's table next to the other's still form. As soon as she locked the wheels with her foot, she bent down, pretending to attend to something in her shoe.

The gray-haired man said nothing as he stalked past Quinn, leaving her alone in the room with the two unconscious candidates.

As soon as he exited the chamber and there was no one else in sight in the passageway, Quinn ducked into the shadows in the corner of the small chamber, waiting for the other cultists to finish filtering back up from the cere-monial chamber. She held off activating her hiding skill until someone came into the room.

As she hid in the deep shadows of chamber's far corner, Quinn ran through her options to get Taylor out of there. She wouldn't leave her best friend behind.

CHAPTER TWENTY

While she waited in the side chamber, Quinn listened to those passing her hiding place. The robed figures chattered idly, most discussions having nothing to do with the failed ceremony below.

The long line of cultists from the ceremonial cavern eventually thinned until it had been several minutes since anyone appeared.

Quinn stepped out of her hiding place and moved over to Taylor's still form on the table. She looked up the passageway leading to the VirSync building above them, then cursed and shook her head. There was no way she could get Taylor out of there without some sort of assistance. She couldn't carry her all the way out alone. Even if she were to somehow get her to awaken, which she couldn't, they'd still have to escape the building and get back to Quinn's Jeep. And that left them inside the walled compound, still likely on lockdown.

Quinn needed help, and there was only one person she knew who could provide it. She pulled out her phone and turned it back on. She waited until it powered up, then held it in the air, checking the signal. The display showed no connection, not even to the building wifi above them.

She was going to have to leave Taylor again and return to the surface to call Clark. Hopefully, he'd have an idea of how to break the spell on the girl, as well as how Quinn could get the two of them out of here.

Quinn returned to the tunnel, looking in both directions as she listened for approaching voices or footsteps. When she was sure no one else was coming, she started back up the tunnel to the elevator.

It didn't take her long. Soon she stood beside the construction elevator looking up the long shaft up to the surface. She could just make out a speck of light at the top. The elevator mechanism was silent, and there were no voices coming down the shaft.

Confident the others had moved away from the elevator above, Quinn pushed the button and stepped back, pressing herself against the side of the shaft so she wasn't in direct view of the elevator when the doors opened. The elevator came down the shaft and opened.

It was empty.

Quinn darted inside just as the elevator doors started to close again and pressed the up button to return to the basement level.

Once again, she tried to hide her presence, standing with her back against the side of the elevator, getting herself out of sight as best she could for when the doors opened at the top. Although she still wore the robes which had served to hide her well enough, it was pressing her luck to rely on them much farther. People on this level would be taking off their robes, and they would expect her to do the same.

When the elevator stopped and the doors opened, she listened carefully. Hearing nothing, Quinn glanced up the short hallway leading to the preparation room.

All clear.

Quinn allowed herself a tiny smile. She just needed to go a bit farther to get a signal.

She moved to the door leading into the preparation room and paused. This was the door that required keycard access from the far side to open.

Quinn expected it to be locked, but when she examined the door from this side, she realized it didn't require a card. All she had to worry about getting back through it after the door locked behind her.

Her ID badge wasn't coded to open it. She'd either need to steal an ID from someone with the correct access or somehow disable the lock in a way that wasn't obvious upon casual examination.

Quinn crouched to examine the mechanism. She'd heard a click when the guy used his keycard earlier to open the door, so the lock must be electromagnetic. Her suspicion was confirmed by a pair of white and black wires coming off the locking mechanism in the wall. The two wires entered a conduit that disappeared into the ceiling.

In theory, if she cut the power to the magnet, it couldn't engage the lock once she went through. Knowing it was all she had to work with, Quinn drew her Bowie knife and set the blade against the two wires.

She drew a deep breath. This was either going to

disable the lock permanently or cause it to trap her on this side.

Committing to her decision, Quinn flicked her wrist, cutting through the two wires with ease. The door clicked and popped open about a quarter inch.

She smiled. With everything stacked against her, it felt good to have even something this small go her way.

Quinn entered the darkened room on the far side and checked her phone.

Two and a half bars.

She nodded. It was enough.

Time to reach out to Clark.

CHAPTER TWENTY-ONE

Outside in the darkened car, Clark's phone buzzed on the dash. It startled him since he was studying the wall across the road, along with the company buildings beyond.

Picking up the phone, he glanced at it. The incoming call came from the forwarded number he'd given Quinn. He tapped Talk.

"Hello, this is Clark."

"Clark, it's Quinn. Thank God! I wasn't sure I'd be able to get an answer at this hour."

"Quinn, where are you?"

"I'm somewhere in the basement of the main building. Listen, I don't have much time."

"No, you don't. You need to get out of there now. The longer you stay in there, the more likely it is you're going to get caught."

"I can't. Not yet. I found something down here. There's a whole system of tunnels below the basement level. They have some sort of ceremonial chamber, and I watched one of them transfer a demon or something into one of the other candidates, taking over his body.

Miranda leaned closer to the phone. "This is Miranda. Tell me exactly what they did as closely as you can."

"They had a red gemstone of some sort that glowed and pulsed during the spell. They called it the Ruby Heart. The leader, CEO Myles Hickman, used it while the others chanted in a group around Fergus. He called it a transference spell. When it was finished, they stopped chanting and the guy on the table sat up, suddenly awakened. He mostly looked normal, but his eyes were completely black. It was like they'd been replaced by black marbles or something."

Miranda nodded. "That gem is very powerful, Quinn. You have to stay away from it. It's a direct connection to the netherworld, and can overcome even the strongest protection spells if it's fully charged."

There was a brief pause on the other end of the line before Quinn continued, "Um, so when they tried to use it on Taylor, I did something. I…"

When the phone went silent for a few seconds, Clark asked, "Quinn, what did you do? Are you all right?"

"I'm fine. I used the power in my amulet to sort of block it, so they drained all its power without making the spell work again."

Clark scowled. "Hold on a second, Quinn. I'll be right back."

He tapped the mute button and looked at Miranda. "Is that even possible? I've never heard of a hunter using their protection magic that way."

Miranda shrugged. "Maybe. At the very least, she thinks

that's what she did. Unmute the connection so I can ask her something.

Clark tapped the button to turn the mic back on and nodded at Miranda.

She leaned closer to the phone and asked, "What do you mean, you did something to it?"

The phone was silent for a few seconds again before Quinn replied, "I honestly don't know what I did specifically. I just remembered Clark saying something about me having inborn abilities that might be awakened by the activation of the amulet's protective power. They were starting to use that gem on Taylor, and I had to try to do something. I tried to refocus the protection the amulet gave me so it extended out and protected her, too."

Miranda's eyebrows shot up. "That should not have even been possible. Tell me exactly what you did. Don't leave anything out."

"What are you thinking she did?" Clark asked.

"I'm not sure. Let her answer."

There was another pause. "I-I don't know. I didn't know it wasn't possible. I pressed down on my amulet while I tried as hard as I could to make it work. It hurt bad. The amulet got so cold, I think it left a mark in my chest. I had to keep trying, no matter what. Then it started working. As I watched, the light in the gemstone dimmed until it stopped altogether and Myles had to cease his spell."

Clark turned from Miranda to the phone. "Myles cast the spell? You're sure?"

"Yes, why?"

"Because I've been trying to figure out who he was ever since I discovered you at VirSync. I did a background check on him, and he doesn't exist before about three years ago. I suspected he was hiding his real identity, and now I'm sure of it."

Miranda nodded. "That makes sense. The strongest of our adversaries disguise themselves in a variety of ways. They also move around a lot to protect themselves. Even with the hunters mostly gone, they've kept the practice going. They've always tried to conceal their true power from the world around them. If this Myles Hickman led the casting of the transference spell, he's likely one of their hidden leaders."

Clark pondered the implications. If what Miranda said was true, Quinn was in even more danger. Even Clark was not prepared to fight with someone with that kind of power.

He picked up the phone off the dash and held it closer. "Look, Quinn, you need to get out of there. This changes everything. It was dangerous enough before. Now it's way beyond that. You can't rescue your friend, and we can't risk losing you. You have to get out."

"I can't leave her down here, Clark. I told you before; I owe her my life. She's unconscious from some sort of spell, and I can't wake her. She has all these runes and symbols drawn all over her."

"You're going to have to leave her, Quinn. You'll have a hard enough time getting out by yourself at this point without having to carry her out unconscious."

"I was hoping maybe you could find a way to get in here and help me or tell me how to wake her up. I can give you directions to exactly where we are."

"I'm not sure I can get past the security at the gate or

over the wall into the facility," Clark said. "Even if I do, there's no guarantee I won't trip the alarm is doing it."

"I might be able to do something about both the magical wards and the mundane security measures like cameras," Miranda said. "While we've been sitting here, I worked out a spell I can use that should, in theory, bypass the alarm system, electrical or magical. I'll have to come with you, though."

"I can't have that," Clark exclaimed. "I'm supposed to be protecting you."

Miranda shook her head. "Right now, we need Quinn. She's important, maybe more important than either of us realizes. I think you know that, too. You heard her describe what she did down there to disrupt the spell. Have you ever known any other hunter with that ability?"

Quinn interrupted, "Please, Clark! I need you to help me get Taylor out of here. I can protect her for now, but I can't move her alone."

Clarke tried to hide the sigh as he realized Miranda was right about the girl's surprising abilities. "All right, Quinn," Clark said. "We'll try. We're not far away, so we'll reach out again once we're safely inside the perimeter and past the outer security wards."

"Good," Quinn said. "While I'm waiting for you, I'm going to try to steal that gem they used for the transference spell."

Clark and Miranda met each other's eyes, alarm crossing their faces. Clark raised the phone until it was inches from his mouth. "Do. Not. Do. That! Do you hear me, Quinn? That gem is a powerful netherworld artifact.

Handling it without knowing how to use it properly or protect yourself could do things to you."

"What kind of things? It didn't seem to hurt Myles. Besides, if I take it, they won't be able to use it to hurt anyone else."

Clark started to say something, but Quinn kept talking, cutting him off.

"You guys get in here so you can help me get Taylor out. I'm going to swipe the gem. Just get into the central building and come down to the basement level in the wing to the right of the main entrance. There's a long hallway. Follow the blue line to the end and take the stairs down. Wait for me at the bottom. I'll be close by."

Clark grumbled, "Quinn, under no circumstances are you to—" He stopped talking and stared at the now-blank phone screen. "She cut me off and hung up. That little…"

Miranda grimaced and said. "She has no idea what that gem could do to her. Based on what she's already done, it's clear she has hidden depths of power we're unaware of. If that gem's what I think it is, it could be sort of self-aware. It would sense her presence when she touches it. It could recognize her as the one who damped its power."

Clark nodded. He tapped the phone and tried to call her back. The call went right to voicemail. "Dammit. She's either ignoring me, or she's moved somewhere she can't get my signal."

"We need to get in there now more than ever." Miranda pointed to the wall. "I think I can neutralize the surveillance systems in a small area and kind of freeze the image for a time, as well as create a small break in the magical wards. At this time of night, they shouldn't notice anything strange on the video monitors if they happen to be looking when I do it. Do you think you can get over that wall and help me follow you?"

Clark nodded. This whole thing was getting out of hand. If they survived, he was going to have a long talk with Quinn about following instructions. In his day, no hunter would disobey a direct order from a superior. He was determined to teach her the right way to do things as he trained her.

Clark slid his phone into the inner pocket of his black overcoat and popped open his door to get out. Miranda hopped out of the passenger side, slinging the strap of her huge purse over her shoulders so it hung across her chest. She nodded, and the two of them crossed the parking lot until they reached the road across from the tall stone wall that protected this part of the VirSync grounds.

Clark pointed to a section that was located as far as possible from nearby lights. "We should try to cross there. Less chance we'll be spotted."

Miranda nodded. "Follow me. I'll dampen the cameras and wards. I don't sense anything terribly complex in that area."

Clark followed her as she started across the street, angling toward the section of the wall he'd indicated.

As they approached it, Miranda raised her arms over her head, stretching them out as far as they would go. She paused in the middle of the road as she muttered something under her breath over and over.

Clark stood behind her, waiting for her spell to take effect. He kept checking the road to make sure there were no headlights coming from either direction.

After about thirty seconds of chanting, she lowered her arms. "It's done. We should be clear almost all the way to the main building. I can check again when we get closer."

Clark nodded and took the lead as they walked up to the base of the wall. He looked up. It was about eight feet to the upper edge.

Clark crouched, then jumped, reaching with both hands for the upper edge. He dug his fingers in, gripping the stone as he pulled himself to the top of the wall.

Swinging a leg over, Clark straddled the wall, then reached down for Miranda's outstretched hand.

She clasped his wrist, and he grabbed hers in turn. Holding tight, he pulled her upward until she could reach the top of the wall with her free hand.

As soon as she scrambled to the top of the wall, Clark turned so he could lower her to the other side. Once she was safely on the ground, he jumped down to land beside her.

They crouched by the wall, staring across the broad swath of close-cut grass toward the corporate buildings about a hundred yards away.

"She said she was in the basement of that one, right?" Miranda pointed to the largest of the four buildings.

Clark nodded. "First, we need to get inside that building without getting detected, then we have to find the stairwell down. Can you handle the security systems like you did the wall?"

"I think I should save my energy for later, just in case. I know you can mask yourself as a hunter. I can use an easier spell to hide myself that'll take a lot less energy than trying to blanket the whole building's security network."

Clark nodded again and they started moving across the grass. About halfway to the main building, Clark activated his ability to draw the shadows around himself. As the familiar haze formed at the edge of his vision, he started walking again.

He looked to his left and right as he moved, searching for Miranda. When he didn't see her, he turned to search behind him.

"I'm right here next to you."

Clark barely resisted the urge to jump and stared at the empty space beside him. He could make out the faint outline of a person if he concentrated.

"Good, I just wanted to make sure you were there. Can you see me?"

"Yes, of course. Yours is based on hiding you from those who don't know you're there."

Clark shrugged and pointed to the main entrance. "Let's try to get in that way. There are enough shadows around with the nighttime lighting scheme inside the building, so we should be able to get pretty close."

He started off, assuming Miranda was with him, stopping when he reached a line of shrubbery next to the sidewalk outside the main entrance.

Clark peered over the bushes and through the glass that covered the front of the building. A single guard sat at a tall information counter about twenty feet inside the entrance.

The uniformed security guy faced the door, but was currently looking down at his lap. He was either dozing or watching something on his phone.

The counter was about chest high, and he sat in a tall chair behind it. It was likely there was a row of monitors behind the counter as well, but they should be mostly protected from casual observation.

The main problem facing them at this point was the bright lighting around the entry doors. It was unlikely the guard would fail to notice the door opening without anyone operating it.

That would cause Clark's personal cloaking to fail rather quickly since the guard would no doubt concentrate his attention on what was making the door move.

He turned to where he could sense Miranda crouching next to him. "I'm not sure we can get all the way to the guard without him seeing us, even with my cloaking and your spell."

Miranda said, "Let me try something."

"What are you going to do?"

"Watch."

Miranda began muttering something as she cast her spell. When he focused on her, her arms seemed to be moving rhythmically. She stopped speaking, and Clark turned to check on the guard.

A few seconds later, the guard stood and rushed from the room toward one of the side halls.

"What did you do? "

"I suggested to his mind that he'd eaten some bad food. It's a simple nausea spell. I came up with it a long time ago to play pranks on my sisters. It's useful here, though, don't you think?"

Clark chuckled. "I'm glad you're on my side. Remind me not to piss you off."

He heard a soprano giggle nearby as he made one last check for more guards before dashing for the front doors.

Miranda beat him there. The door opened just ahead of his reaching hand and he ran through, turned to the right, and headed for the shadows by a concrete pillar.

He stopped as Miranda asked from behind him, "Which way?"

"It should be to the right of the main entrance if what Quinn said was correct. We have to be careful, though. There are probably still others here since she said the transference ceremony just took place."

The two of them hurried past the empty security desk, bearing to the right until they found the double doors leading to the hall Quinn had described.

The long corridor had lines painted on the floor in red, blue, and green. Every third panel in the overhead lights was lit, which kept Clark's masking ability working to its fullest.

He and Miranda started moving down the hallway, following the lines. He stayed pressed against the right-hand wall keeping his wrap of shadows around himself. He should be nearly invisible if someone came into the hallway ahead of them.

The green line turned left first, disappearing through doors labeled Chemical Receiving.

The red line turned off next, heading through doors to the right. Since that was the correct side of the building for finding Quinn, he tried the doors.

They were locked.

Miranda said, "She said to follow the blue line, remember? Come on, this way."

Clark started to follow her just as he heard voices

coming from behind the locked doors. "People are coming. Let's get to that stairwell."

Clark started down the hallway, following the blue line as he moved away from the doors. There were several doors at the end of the hall, but he couldn't make out what they were or where they led. He assumed one led to a stairwell, as Quinn had told them.

Behind him, the red doors opened, and about a dozen men and women exited and turned toward the main lobby.

He froze and hugged the wall, hoping his masking ability held up in the shadows halfway between the overhead lights.

The group continued toward the entrance without looking back. None noticed Clark or Miranda.

He waited until the last of them went through the doors to the lobby before he checked around to find Miranda.

The sound of her voice much farther down the hall surprised him.

"There's a gym down here, and a stairwell door, too."

Clark jogged that way but froze in place as more voices echoed from the stairwell. They were laughing loudly.

Clark looked around and then pointed at the other door, the one to the gym. "Quick, in here."

Clark pushed the door open and saw a faint blur as Miranda moved past him. He darted in just as another group came through the stairwell door.

Inside the gym, Clark spotted a small storage closet and checked the doorknob.

It was unlocked.

He pulled it open and pushed Miranda's hazy form

inside, following her in as the door to the gym opened behind them.

Voices filled the outer room as the group of men grumbled about some ceremony that had failed, requiring them to return the following day. They all sounded like they planned on staying to work out for a while.

Clark and Miranda stood face to face, pressed very close together inside the awkward confines of the closet. He let his masking ability drop as Miranda cleared her spell. They avoided each other's eyes as they waited for the men using the weight room and gym equipment outside to leave.

As he waited, trapped inside the closet, Clark's thoughts turned to Quinn. He hoped she was being smart.

Somehow he knew otherwise.

CHAPTER TWENTY-TWO

Quinn hung up from the call with Clark. She knew all he was going to do was yell at her, and she didn't need some old guy to tell her it was a risk to go after the gem on top of everything else she needed to do. She wasn't an idiot.

Her problem was, it was the only way she could think of to stop them from continuing to use it to possess people.

Quinn started toward the elevator down to the tunnels. She couldn't be sure all the cultists from the ceremony had returned. It seemed as if most, if not all of them, had left for the night. If any were still down there, she'd have to deal with them.

After taking the elevator down, Quinn stepped into the tunnel and headed back down it. She stopped briefly in the side chamber, where Taylor and the other candidate remained comatose on their respective tables.

Quinn went in and laid a hand on Taylor's arm. She was freezing cold but still breathing steadily. Quinn considered finding a robe or a blanket to drape over her friend's body. She couldn't afford anyone seeing it, though. They'd know someone was down here who didn't belong.

Quinn sighed, returned to the passage, and made her way to the ceremonial cavern. She moved slowly, taking her time and listening for voices or footsteps. The smooth stone floor made it easy for her to move quietly, but that also meant others could do so as well.

She paused for a few seconds and tried to use her amulet's power to help her hide. It didn't work.

Quinn wasn't surprised. She'd used a lot of energy blocking the spell attempting to possess Taylor.

The amulet wasn't the only thing that needed to recharge. The pit in Quinn's stomach reminded her of how hungry she was.

The sandwich! There was one more in her gym bag, which was slung beneath her robe.

Quinn opened the robe and retrieved one of the two water bottles and the remaining sandwich.

She stopped at a bend in the passage and wolfed down the Kaiser roll filled with turkey and cheese. She ate so fast, she barely tasted it.

Quinn chugged the water, washing the last crumbs of the sandwich down with it. Her hunger pangs hadn't disappeared completely, but she definitely felt better.

She thought about trying her hiding ability again but decided against it. It would use energy she might need later. If it worked, it was best to save its limited duration for a moment when she really needed it.

As she started downward again, Quinn wondered what other abilities or powers she possessed that might be enabled or awakened by the amulet. She should have gotten Clark to tell her more about them.

It could be almost anything. Did she have super strength? Could she draw on some sort of stamina reserves to increase her physical capabilities? It was something to consider.

Quinn was so lost in thought, she almost stumbled into the cultist standing guard at the entrance to the ceremonial chamber.

She stopped herself just in time and stepped back around the final bend in the tunnel before she was spotted.

Luckily, the guy in the robes wasn't looking her way. He seemed to be watching the center of the chamber. The flames from the brazier left the room with a flickering orange and yellow light that cast strange shadows on the walls.

Quinn wondered what fueled the fire for it to keep it burning like that. The basin at the top of the pedestal wasn't that large, and the coals in it should have burned out by now.

Perhaps the person standing guard here was tasked with feeding fuel to the fire. Of course, it could also have some sort of magical origin. Either would make sense.

Quinn peeked around the corner and studied the guy. It was definitely a male, judging by height. She couldn't tell otherwise because the hood on his robe was up, just as hers was.

Quinn decided to try something risky. If it worked, it would avoid a potentially noisy fight. She was pretty sure she could take the guy, especially if she caught him by surprise, but that might raise some sort of an alarm, and she couldn't tell if any other cultists remained inside the cavern.

Taking a deep breath, Quinn clasped her hands in front of her, bowed her head in what she hoped was a reverent pose, and turned the corner. She walked with confident strides toward the chamber. She made it a point to not disguise her steps, scuffing her feet on the stone floor on purpose.

The cultist below turned in her direction right away. "What's up? Did you forget something?"

Quinn lowered her voice in an attempt to disguise it. "I was sent to relieve you. Since you all contributed blood to recharging the gem, I was told to take the next shift watching the chamber."

Quinn tensed, ready to attack if her ruse failed.

Relief flooded through her when the guy said, "Oh, that's great. I was having trouble keeping my eyes open. The giving of blood and energy like that saps so much strength."

"Glad I could be of service. Why don't you go get some rest? I've got this."

The cultist didn't wait for Quinn to reach his place by the cavern's entrance. He rushed past her after a brief nodded thank you.

Quinn took up the position where he'd been standing and watched him go around the bend in the tunnel. As soon as he was out of sight, she let out a long, slow breath, then stretched and flexed to remove some of the tension in her muscles. She'd been ready to attack and disable him or worse. Quinn had only half-believed this plan would work.

She waited for a few long minutes to ensure he'd

returned to the surface before she moved on with the rest of her plan. Quinn checked the passage one last time, walking up to the bend to check the portion beyond.

It was clear.

Smiling, Quinn returned and entered the cavern, heading straight to the burning brazier in the center of the room. The gemstone was still perched on a brass plate over the coals. It pulsed with a sickening, bloody-red color deep in its core.

Quinn's nose wrinkled at the residual sickly-sweet odor that she realized was from the blood shed by the cultists to recharge the gem's power. She didn't know what would make people do something like that.

She pulled the sleeve of her robe over her hand to protect her from the heat and reached out to grab it from the plate in the center of the flaming brazier. An wave of revulsion instantly swept over her, stopping her hand before it got close to the Ruby Heart.

Quinn took a step back as she almost vomited right there next to the pedestal.

Bent over and gulping air, she steeled herself to push through the sickening sensation.

After gathering her resolve, Quinn straightened and reached out again. This time she snatched the gem quickly, grabbing it before nausea set in again.

The moment she lifted the gem from the brass plate, Quinn's amulet sent a powerful chill through her. The evil nature of the artifact assaulted her, and her hunter protections fired up as soon as she touched it, even through the cloth of her robe's sleeve.

Guttural whispers came from all around her as she dropped it in her pocket.

It was as if the gem was alive somehow, just as Miranda had warned her. She could sense its desire to exert control over her as soon as she touched it. She was glad it was hot enough that she hadn't wanted to use her bare hands. That might help her get away with this in the long run.

The whispering voices grew louder now that the gem was in her pocket. She could make out parts of the muttered suggestions.

They all wanted her to do things, horrible things.

Quinn squeezed her eyes shut and took several deep breaths to try to clear her mind of the suggestions, but the whispers continued to pass through the back of her mind. They told her to do everything from thrusting her free hand into the brazier's flames just to see what charred skin looked and smelled like to returning back up to passage and snapping Taylor's neck.

For a split second, it seemed as if the voices would win. Quinn focused on the icy chill against her breastbone, and to her happy surprise, the whispering stopped.

The experience left her flustered, though, and she considered putting the gem back and giving up on her plan to steal it.

She stood by the pedestal for nearly thirty seconds, trying to make up her mind.

In the end, she shook her head and said aloud, "No, this has to be done. I have to go through with this before others are turned.

Quinn turned back toward the cavern's main entrance. As she did, voices echoed down the tunnel from up ahead.

A lot of voices. It sounded like way more than just a few people.

Spinning around, Quinn searched for a place to hide and spotted two other openings, narrow, unworked cracks in the cavern walls. They looked like they led from the cavern, heading deeper into the network of caves beneath the company buildings.

Quinn didn't have much time to make a decision about which way to go. The people behind those voices had almost reached the cavern.

She ran to the right, darting out of sight through the closest of the two dark openings as a group of six cultists, led by Myles Hickman, entered the room.

All of them wore street clothes, except for the guy she'd relieved from guard duty and two others she couldn't make out. Quinn crouched in the shadows just inside the crack in the wall and watched to see what they did. Perhaps they'd think she'd headed back up to the building.

"The gem," Myles exclaimed, pointing at the empty plate on the brazier. "It's gone."

"My Lord," the tall man Quinn had relieved said. "I had no reason to believe she was anything but one of us when she offered to take over for me."

"I'll deal with you later. She couldn't have gone far. Search back up the main tunnel. See if she's hiding in a crack or crevice somewhere. She didn't come back up the elevator, so she has to be down here somewhere."

Two women at the back of the group turned and ran back up the corridor, heading for the surface to search for Quinn. Two others turned toward Myles. As soon as they turned around, Quinn recognized them.

Cindy and Fergus studied Myles for a few seconds, then turned their black eyes to search the rest of the cavern.

Cindy lifted her head as if sniffing the air. "The gem is near. I can sense its presence. She has not gone far. I do not think she's heading toward the surface."

Cindy's black eyes continued scanning the walls.

Fergus spoke as well. "There is something else. Something old and familiar. I sense hunter magic."

Myles barked an uncomfortable laugh. "That's impossible. The hunters are all gone. Even if any of that ilk remain alive, there are none who would dare come here and attack us in the our center of power."

Cindy stopped scanning the cavern and shifted her gaze back to Myles. "My comrade is correct. I didn't sense it at first, but it is there. It is faint, as if colored by something else. Nonetheless, it is definitely hunter magic."

Myles blanched at the pronouncement. "I assure you, we will find her and do with her what we did with the rest of her kind years ago."

Cindy had returned to scanning the cavern, her black eyes approaching the place Quinn hid. She didn't dare use her hiding ability for fear it would increase their sense of her magic nearby.

In the end, it didn't matter.

Cindy's arm snapped up, finger pointing directly at Quinn.

"There!"

Myles and the acolyte who had been guarding the chamber before ran toward the opening where Quinn hid.

She scrambled backward and turned, working her way

farther into the narrow gap and scraping her exposed skin as she pulled herself over the rough surface.

As she went back, it quickly became pitch-black. She tried to navigate by feel alone, but knew she needed to go faster.

Quinn tried to activate her night vision ability but nothing happened. She scrambled to remember what she'd done back in the room with the other candidates.

Her mind rolled through the earlier part of the evening until it came to her. As she crawled through the darkness, trying to get away from those coming, she whispered, "Dammit, I need to see."

Instantly, the familiar bluish hue from before lit the narrow passageway. Quinn smiled despite the desperate nature of the situation. Those were probably not the words Clark would have trained her to use, but they worked well enough, and they suited her.

Now that she could see where she was going, Quinn picked up speed. She moved as fast as she dared while trying to remain silent. The rough tunnel opened up at times enough that she could stand upright. At other times, though, it narrowed to the point where she wriggled along on her belly.

The voices of Myles and the other cultists echoed through the caves behind her. She was sure they hadn't seen her, but clearly they trusted Cindy's sense of smell or whatever she'd used to detect Quinn's presence.

When Quinn glanced behind her and saw the flash-lights illuminating the path of her pursuers.

She reached a point where two passages branched off. One sloped down, and the other angled to the left and ran gently upward. There was also a pool of water roughly the size of a big jacuzzi tub off to one side.

Quinn knew it was likely she'd get stuck in here or hit a dead end, and then they'd find her. She worried what would happen when they caught her and retrieved the gem. She'd never be able to overcome four of them at once, and she was sure they'd use it to bring a demon into her body.

Making up her mind, Quinn pulled the now-cool gemstone from her pocket, once again using the sleeve of her robe to keep from touching it directly.

Swallowing the bile that rose in her throat, Quinn went to the pool of dark water and tossed the gem into the far corner.

The pulsing red stone sank, slowly fading from view.

The voices grew louder behind her, and Quinn glanced back again. They'd almost reached this area. Making a snap decision, Quinn took the passage that sloped upward. Maybe she'd be lucky, and it would come out on the surface somewhere close by. If that was the case, she could get out and possibly still find a way to get back in to rescue Taylor.

Quinn scrambled upward. The passage continued for about a hundred yards before it narrowed to the point that Quinn could go no farther. A distinct draft of fresh air came through the narrow gap ahead of her, but unless she could transform herself into a mouse or a rat, she wasn't getting out that way.

Desperation gave way to despair. She was so close.

Turning back, Quinn started in the other direction.

Hopefully, Myles and the others had opted to search the other passage, leaving her a way to slip past them.

The movement of lights ahead of her told her she was not going to be so lucky. Someone was coming this way.

Quinn searched for a place to hide. Seeing none, she pressed herself against the wall near a bend in tunnel. Maybe if she caught them by surprise, she could attack them one by one.

It was her only chance.

CHAPTER TWENTY-THREE

Judging by the grunts of effort emanating from it, someone was in the process of coming through the rough crack she'd emerged from moments before.

The beam of a flashlight preceded the robed arm of the cultist guard she'd relieved of duty earlier.

Quinn waited until the tall, lanky guy had almost crawled completely through the opening before she pounced on him from her hiding place above and behind him.

Still unwilling to kill anyone, she reversed her grip on the Bowie knife's hilt so she could lead with the pommel. She landed with her feet straddling the cultist and brought the pommel down hard on the back of his head.

He let out a soft groan, spasmed once, and lay still.

Praying he wasn't dead, Quinn grabbed him by the waist and rolled him out of the way. Once he was free of the opening, she shoved the unconscious form with her foot to roll him down a short slope to land wedged against the slanted wall.

Quinn returned to the opening, resumed her position, and waited to see if anyone else came through.

No one did.

Instead, a few seconds later, Myles called through the gap. "Rutherford, where are you? Is she in there?"

Quinn started to answer but realized she'd never fool them into thinking she was the unconscious cultist. Instead, she stayed put and readied herself to fight whoever came through to check on the first guy.

"Rutherford, are you there?" Myles repeated his question.

Another flashlight beam shone through the hole, moving around and illuminating the far wall of the cave. Given the narrow opening, Quinn knew they couldn't see much.

Cindy's voice, tainted by the demonic undertone Quinn had heard in Fergus's voice at the ceremony, came from inside the narrow passageway, "I'll go through and find out what's wrong with your underling. If she truly is a hunter, she'll be more formidable than you lot can handle."

The woman wormed her way through the opening until Quinn saw her head emerge from the crack.

Once again, Quinn waited until Cindy was most of the way through before attacking. The plan was to repeat her attack and stash her with Rutherford.

That turned out to be a bad idea.

Possessed Cindy was much stronger and faster than Quinn.

Quinn jumped down as she had before, straddling the woman's torso.

This time, however, Cindy twisted in an unbelievable,

back-cracking motion and rolled over before Quinn could react. The black eyes bored into hers and the possessed woman punched upward with both hands before Quinn's descending attack even got close to her.

The blow propelled Quinn off the ground and slammed her into the jagged rocks of the tunnel's ceiling eight feet above. Her knife flew from her hand to clatter to the floor nearby.

By the time Quinn fell back to the ground, Cindy had continued her roll to the side and sprung to her feet with impossible speed.

Quinn's feet scrabbled at the loose rocks on the cave floor as she tried to get up.

The other woman took a step toward Quinn and landed a kick at her midsection. The blow struck hard enough to knock the wind out of her, as well as send her tumbling to slam into Rutherford's still form.

Shaking her head to clear the cobwebs after the stunning attacks, Quinn struggled again to get to her feet.

Cindy pounced on Quinn before she could get up, kneeling above her so her knees pinned Quinn's arms to her sides.

Then the possessed woman rained blows on Quinn's unprotected head and face while she cackled with evil glee.

A voice sounded from the cave opening. "Enough! Get the gem from her first, then you can do as you please."

Quinn turned her dazed and bloody head toward the entrance. Myles had crawled partway through the opening and now shone his flashlight across the sloped floor at them.

Hands began digging through her clothing and into the

gym bag beneath her robe, searching through pockets real or imagined for many long seconds.

Quinn's groggy mind struggled to reset and find a way to get free. Her feeble attempts to resist were met with two quick punches to her gut, leaving her gasping for breath again.

Cindy snarled as she finished her search. "There's nothing but this cell phone and car keys, plus some clothes in a bag."

"Drag her up here to the opening and we'll pull her through," Myles said. "We'll search her again on this side."

"What do you want me to do with your underling?"

"Leave him, but take his flashlight. If he can find his way out on his own, he might be worth keeping around. Otherwise, he'll die as he deserves."

Quinn was rolled over until she was face-down. Cindy wrenched her arms backward until her wrist crossed. Something was wrapped around her wrists and pulled tight, then Cindy shoved her into the opening head-first. Other hands grabbed her shoulders and pulled her through to the larger area on the other side.

Two people lifted Quinn to her feet, holding her in place when she swayed and began to fall.

She lifted her head, struggling to bring everything into focus. Flashlights shone into her eyes, blinding her so she couldn't see much more than a cluster of shadows around her.

Finally, the lights moved away, and Quinn blinked away the purple dots swimming in her eyes.

In front of her stood Myles Hickman, CEO of VirSync

and the high priest of this evil clan of demonic cultists or whatever they were.

Quinn, frustrated by her capture, finally found her voice. She shouted at him, "Let me go."

Myles smiled. "Oh, my dear, there is no reason for me to release you. You have caused quite a bit of disturbance since you came here."

He turned his attention to those holding her. "Search her again. Find the gem."

Quinn struggled again to no avail as hands patted her down, searching her pockets. They removed the robe and searched her jeans pockets, too.

They were not gentle. When the one on her left groped her breasts during the search, she stomped hard on the guy's foot.

This earned her a punch in the gut that bent her over with a groan.

Quinn had trouble standing upright again to face her captors. Her battered body was starting to fail her.

"We can't find it, my lord. She doesn't have it on her."

Myles nodded and returned his attention to Quinn. "Where is it? Where is the Ruby Heart?"

"I don't know what you're talking about. I got turned around and got lost down here."

"Nonsense. You've been working against our purposes since you arrived. It's the only thing that makes sense. You're the only candidate who failed to complete the missions or make a kill. Did the woman you were chasing really fall into the harbor, or was that just a story you made up after you helped her escape?"

Quinn couldn't resist the smile that spread across her

face. "Wouldn't you like to know?"

Myles' expression darkened. "That type of insolence will not help you in this situation, my dear. Tell me what you did with the gem. That is the only thing that will improve your fate."

Quinn forced a laugh. "Do you expect me to believe anything is going to change if I tell you where that gem of yours is? I have a good idea about what you have in store for me. I've seen what you do to people down here."

She stared at Cindy and Fergus, who both returned her gaze with their pitch-black eyes.

"You saw that, did you?" Myles asked with a broad grin. "We are merely fulfilling our unholy charge. These are but the vanguard of a whole army of warriors from the netherworld who will come into this land. Eventually, we will replace the leadership of every country with those who follow us or with possessed shells. Then there will be no one to resist us."

"Do you really think that's going to work? Don't you think people will notice folks walking around with pitch-black eyes like theirs? Look at them." Quinn pointed at Cindy and Fergus. "When someone sees them like that, they're going to shoot first and ask questions later."

"I think you will find our possessed fellows are far more formidable than mere humans. Once brought through the portal to invest in a human body, the netherworlders are able to significantly strengthen the weak physical form that is the human body. As they assimilate to our world and their hosts, over time, they will master their vessels, and the eyes will return to normal. No one will be able to see the difference."

"The hunters will know."

The statement produced the first crack in Myles's confidence.

"How do you know about the hunters? You're not old enough to have been around during the purge."

Quinn smiled. "I know the hunters aren't as dead as you think they are. I know the hunters are converging even now on this place. They've found you, and once they've gathered their strength, your little plan for world domination is over."

Myles gazed into Quinn's eyes as if trying to determine the truth of what she'd said.

"You're bluffing."

"Am I? You said it yourself. I shouldn't know anything about the hunter clans. Did you really think you'd manage to get all of them in your so-called purge?"

Fergus turned to Myles. "You assured our masters the hunter clans were no longer a threat."

"She's lying, can't you see that? She's stalling to keep us from killing her outright."

Cindy said, "Until we ascertain the truth of her words, we must keep her for further questioning. This does not bode well for our plans on this plane, priest. There are those below who need to hear of it."

Myles paused before nodding to the demon-possessed candidates.

"Very well. We will hold her for now without killing her. She's lying. I know it. But there is no harm in keeping her alive until you're both satisfied we're not in any danger." Myles pointed to the two cultists holding her. "Take her up to the basement level. Restrain her in one of the rooms there, and guard her until further notice. Do not leave that door unattended for any reason. Do you understand?"

The man to Quinn's right nodded. "Yes, my lord."

Quinn smiled at Myles and didn't try to resist as they pulled her back down the passage toward the ceremonial chamber.

Myles paid her no attention as she was dragged away, instead turning his gaze upon several other cultists who had shown up to join the search. "Don't just stand there. Search this entire passage. She must've hidden the gem in here somewhere. Find it, or so help me, I'll make you all the next candidates for transference."

A chorus sounded from the group. "Yes, my lord."

The two male cultists holding Quinn continued to pull her down the rough tunnel. She knew she had to try to break their grip. Then she might have a chance to run back up the passage before they caught her. She'd figure out how to cut her hands loose later.

They weren't stupid. Her captors were ready for her.

As soon as Quinn jerked her arms to pull free, the one to her right punched her in the gut again.

The air rushed out of her as she groaned at the pain and doubled over between them, meeting the rising knee of the other cultist, which cracked into Quinn's forehead so hard she blacked out for a split second.

Her captors held her up until her legs started working again. The one on her left said, "Stop struggling, or we'll knock you out and carry you the rest of the way."

For a second, Quinn almost dared him to do it, but she realized he had no compunction about not injuring her.

She'd merely end up unconscious and trapped. At least if she was awake, she'd know where they'd taken her. She had to trust there'd be another opportunity to get loose and find a way out.

The pair hauled Quinn back to the ceremonial chamber, past the glowing brazier, and up the long tunnel that led to the elevator. And she passed the alcove with Taylor's body, Quinn glanced inside to see if her friend was still there.

She was.

There were several other cultists in there with her, standing around the two tables where she and the other naked candidate lay, ready for another ceremony.

Quinn knew it would happen if she didn't figure a way to get Taylor out of here. They'd find the gem sooner or later. She had to get free as quickly as possible.

When they reached the elevator, they pushed her inside, shoving her from behind so she slammed painfully into the metal grid on the far side. Her escorts laughed, pulled the elevator doors closed, and punched the button to return them to the basement above.

Once they were on that level, they took Quinn through the preparation room and back through the long corridor. About a third of the way down, they stopped at one of the doors with a card reader and a lock mounted on the door.

"This one will do." The cultist pulled a keycard from his pants pocket and used it to unlock the door.

The other one shoved her between the shoulder blades so she stumbled into the small storeroom with shelves along the walls.

Quinn banged against the metal shelves against the far

wall before she regained her balance. She turned to glare at the two as they shut the door.

Trying to see where she was, Quinn activated her night vision ability. "Dammit, I need to see."

As soon as she spoke the words, the room became visible.

There were no other exits. The shelves held cleaning supplies, and a mop and a wheeled bucket stood in the corner.

Quinn knew her captors were just outside. She had to remain silent while she tried to free herself.

She sat down and stretched her arms out behind her to pass her bound hands beneath her feet.

Quinn grunted through the pain as the bindings twisted and dug into her wrists while she performed the maneuver. She finally stretched her arms enough to bring them to the front.

Ignoring the pain and bloody cuts on her wrists, Quinn examined the thick plastic zip-ties that bound her wrists. They were too thick to break using brute strength, so she started looking for something she could use to cut through the plastic.

Getting back to her feet, Quinn searched the room in earnest. There had to be something in here she could use. Scanning each of the shelves in turn, Quinn finally found something that might do the trick.

The old rusted metal putty knife had fallen behind the shelf on the right. She managed to move enough of the containers out of the way to reach in and pull it free.

Quinn examined the broad, flat blade. The edge was

dull and rusty, and had definitely seen better days. It would probably do the trick, though, given enough time.

Sitting on the floor with her knees bent and her feet flat on the ground, Quinn placed the plastic handle between her feet so she could hold it steady. She pressed the plastic tie against it with the thin metal blade between her palms.

Quinn started sliding her hands back and forth, pressing the plastic ties against the metal blade. It hurt her injured wrists, but she gritted her teeth against the pain as she applied pressure.

Quinn kept at it for several minutes and finally managed to snap the first of the thick plastic ties. Nearly free, Quinn worked on the second one until it, too, broke.

She rubbed her sore wrist, examining the places where the plastic had gouged her skin. The bleeding wasn't very bad and would probably stop on its own. It didn't appear to have done any permanent injury. She was more worried about what her battered face looked like, and whether she had a concussion from the beating Cindy had given her.

Turning her attention back to the contents of the tiny room, Quinn focused on finding some way to give herself an advantage so she could break free.

She assumed Clark and Miranda had come after her. When they did, they'd run right into a potential trap. She needed to get loose and warn them the cultists were still here in force.

Looking around at the contents of the room, a plan started forming as she took stock of what she had available.

CHAPTER TWENTY-FOUR

S he didn't rush because she had to be careful. She didn't want to make any noise that might alert the guards outside the door she was up to something, or that she'd freed her hands.

When she'd finished her search, Quinn scanned every shelf, remembering what was on each of them.

There were numerous bottles of cleaning chemicals. She'd initially considered using them to try to create some kind of chemical bomb or gas but decided that was a bad idea. She had not been much of a chemistry or science student in school, and she figured she'd be just as likely to injure herself as the guards.

In the end, the only things Quinn found that could approximate a weapon were the paint scraper and the wooden mop handle. She unscrewed the handle from the mop head, then, using a nearly empty roll of packing tape, Quinn attached the scraper.

The resulting weapon looked like it would only be

dangerous to a large can of putty or plaster, but it was all she had.

Quinn was working through her plan of attack when the door opened behind her, spilling bright light into the room.

She spun, whipping the mop handle around to brandish the flat scraper edge at the open doorway.

A laughing voice met her lunge as a hand batted away the poor excuse for a weapon.

"What are you going to do with that, kid?" Clark asked, his tall form casting a shadow into the room.

Upon hearing his voice, Quinn relaxed as relief flooded through her. "Thank God you're here. Is Miranda with you?"

The female sorceress stepped into view. "I'm here."

"Good! Hey, where did the two—" Quinn began, stepping into the hallway. The two cultists stood there next to Miranda, staring at Quinn without moving.

The sight of them startled her for a split second. She almost launched a roundhouse kick at the one who'd punched her in the gut twice, but she managed to regain control.

"What did you do to those two?"

Miranda smiled. "I froze them in a time bubble. It'll fade in ten to fifteen minutes and they won't remember any of us being here. If we close the door, they'll think you're still inside."

"Nice trick." Quinn turned to Clark. "They've got Taylor down below under some sort of spell. I can't make her wake up, but maybe you or Miranda can."

"Wait a minute," Clark said, holding up a hand to slow

Quinn down. "We risked everything to come in here to get you. We're not going to traipse around to rescue your friend, too."

"That's the only reason I came back. I told you that from the beginning. I'm not leaving without her."

For a few seconds, Clark stared at her. Quinn met his glare, her eyes as steely as his.

He tried to loom over her as if he could scare her into doing as he said. She bristled at him and opened her mouth to tell him what he could do with his orders.

Clark started to say something at the same time.

Before either of them could shout at the other, Miranda stepped between them. "Settle down, both of you. We're not going to get anywhere arguing about this, and we can't stay here in the midst of these animals anyway. I don't have much energy left, and from the look of your face, Quinn, you are about finished, too."

"I can still get the job done. Don't worry about me."

Miranda held up her hand to stop Quinn. "How far away is she?"

Quinn pointed down the corridor to the door at the end of the hall. "Through there is an elevator leading down to a system of tunnels and caves below the building. She's being held down there. It's not far."

"Was that where you saw the ceremonial chamber and the gem?" Miranda asked.

Quinn nodded. "That part is much farther down the tunnel. There are eight to ten of the cultists down there, based on what I saw on my way up. I think they'll be busy for a while since I took their precious Ruby Heart and put it somewhere it'll be hard to find. If we go right now, we should be able to get to Taylor and the other one and get back out before they come to check on her."

Miranda glanced at Clark.

The hunter let out an exasperated sigh. "Fine. Let's get moving. We need to be on the way out of here five minutes ago."

He started toward the door at the end of the corridor, but Quinn stopped him.

"Wait, we need something first."

She ran to the room with all the robes, grabbed two of them, and returned to where Miranda and Clark stood waiting.

"What are they for?" Clark asked.

"You'll see." She pointed at the two catatonic cultists who'd been guarding the door. "What about them?

Miranda laughed. "We'll be out of here before they wake up if Taylor is as close as you say."

"Hurry up," Clark said as he started down the hallway again. "This is taking too long."

The three of them moved down the corridor and entered the preparation room. Quinn led the way and they passed through the other door, walking down the short corridor to the elevator down to the caves.

As they waited for the elevator to come up the long shaft, Quinn glanced at Miranda. "Can you teach me how to do that spell you used on those two guys upstairs? Something like that might come in handy."

Miranda smiled. "I told you when we first met, that type of spell casting is not something everyone can do. If you have the affinity for it, I'll be able to teach you something, though. We'll see once we're somewhere safe."

Clark turned to Quinn, saying, "Describe to me exactly what it looks like at the bottom of this elevator. I need to be ready in case there's anyone there."

Quinn told him about the sloping passage with the different alcoves branching off it, including the one that held the two captives.

"That's where the two are being held. There were several cultists in there with them when they brought me up."

"I'll be ready for them," Miranda said. "Clark, you worry about anyone coming up the tunnel. As long as we catch them by surprise, I should be able to deal with anyone who's still in with Quinn's friends."

Clark nodded. He reached under his long, dark overcoat and drew out a short, slightly curved sword.

Quinn stared at it. "Don't you have a gun or something? I thought you were a hunter!"

Clark shook his head. "They will have protections that can deal with mundane weapons, including firearms. This sword has magic of its own that both protects me and makes it more useful in combat against our adversaries. It will counter most of those types of spells, and will also serve well against any possessed by demons."

"I hope so. They're strong. Stronger than a normal human."

Clark offered her a grim smile. "Sounds like you found out the hard way. I wondered how you got so banged up."

"She caught me by surprise, that's all. I'll get the better of her the next time."

"There won't be next time, or at least, not any time

soon. You need training before you go up against any of the possessed alone."

Quinn started to open her mouth to argue but shut it. Little Cindy had smacked her around pretty good without much effort. She didn't want to admit it, but maybe she *did* need to learn a little something before she got payback.

The elevator doors opened, and the trio started the journey to the caverns.

Clark had them all stand against one wall as the car approached the bottom. Hopefully, no one standing in the corridor would see them right away.

The doors opened, and Quinn tensed for a fight. Luckily for them, there was no one there.

Clark held a finger to his lips and pointed down the tunnel while he looked at Quinn.

She led them down the passage and pointed to the bend in the sloping path where the alcove was.

Whispering, Quinn said, "That's where they're holding her. Just go around that bend, and the chamber is right there."

Clark nodded and glanced at Miranda, who smiled and gestured to the tunnel.

He headed down the tunnel, his sword at the ready in front of him. As they approached the alcove, Clark slowed and pointed to Miranda.

She slipped in front of him and edged against the wall close to the opening.

Clark trained his eyes on the tunnel beyond, watching for others.

Quinn heard a soft whisper, and the amulet flared cold on her chest. Miranda's lips moved, although barely any sound came out. She lifted her hands in front of her, fingers weaving an intricate pattern, then took a bold step forward to stand in the alcove's opening and pressed her hands forward. She said the word "sleep."

Something clattered to the stone floor inside the chamber. Quinn darted around the sorceress, ready for a fight. Two cultists lay unconscious on the floor. Another groaned and held his head in his hands, shaking it as if he were trying to clear his mind.

Quinn didn't wait for Miranda to say anything. She scooped up a loose stone from the chamber's entrance and brought it down hard on the third guy's head.

He staggered to the side but didn't go down.

She had to hit him two more times before he fell to the floor and stayed there.

Taylor and the other candidate still lay naked on their tables.

Quinn turned to Miranda. "Can you wake them?"

"Let me see what they did to them. I've never seen this before."

Miranda moved forward, one hand raised in front of her. She began sketching patterns in the air again as she muttered words in a strange language.

Quinn went to stand next to Taylor as Miranda cast her spell. The sorceress stepped forward and lowered her hands until her thumbs pressed against Taylor's forehead on either side.

Behind them, Clark hissed, "Hurry up. I hear voices."

Miranda nodded. "I can wake her, but there's not enough time to wake the other one too, Quinn."

Quinn glanced at the other candidate, knowing what was in store for him if they couldn't take him along.

While Quinn stood there worrying about the other guy, Miranda finished her spell.

Taylor gasped and sat up.

Quinn grabbed her by the shoulders and moved to stand in front of her. "Taylor, look at me. Don't look anywhere else, just at me."

Taylor's wide eyes darted around, trying to see beyond Quinn. She opened her mouth, drawing a big breath.

Quinn clamped a hand over Taylor's mouth before she could let out a yell.

Taylor began to struggle, but Quinn held on. She bent over so she was right next to Taylor's ear. "It's me. It's Quinn. You're all right. Just don't yell, or you'll give us away."

"Hurry up," Clark hissed. He'd backed up so he was standing in the entrance to the alcove. "The voices are coming closer."

"Taylor, don't yell. Got it?"

Taylor nodded, and Quinn removed her hand.

The naked girl threw her hands across her chest, covering what she could. "What the hell is going on, Quinn? Where are my clothes?"

"It's a long story. Here, put this on, and we'll explain once we're away from here."

Quinn handed her friend one of the robes she'd brought down.

Taylor slipped the robe on and stood up. "Where's here?"

"There's no time for that, Taylor. We need to get out of here."

Taylor followed Quinn's instructions, buttoning up the robe.

Miranda moved to Taylor's other side, and together, she and Quinn hustled the other girl back up the tunnel toward the elevator. Clark came right behind them.

A shout came from down the tunnel. Quinn looked over her shoulder.

They'd been seen.

Myles, Cindy, Fergus, and several other cultists came around the bend behind them.

The high priest pointed at Quinn and the others. "Stop them."

Quinn let go of Taylor's arm. "Miranda, get her to the elevator and take her upstairs. We'll be right up."

Miranda nodded and tugged at the dazed Taylor to keep her moving.

Quinn moved over to stand next to Clark.

He started to say something to her, then shook his head and reached into his trench coat. He pulled a long, triangular dagger from inside.

"Here. Try not to cut your fingers off."

"What if I kill one of them?"

"They're already damned. Your soul is safe."

She smiled and took the knife. She wanted payback.

Clark dodged the first of the cultists racing up the passage and swept his blade around, cutting the man deep across the chest.

The guy shrieked in agony and spun away, clutching the bloody gash running diagonally from shoulder to hip.

Clark moved to the next target with a flowing efficiency that surprised Quinn, given his age.

She tore her eyes away from Clark's fluid fighting motions. Cindy had moved into position and snarled as she ran at Quinn.

Remembering the short redhead's surprising strength earlier, Quinn wished she could draw on her stamina the way she had inside the VR system.

To her surprise, a green status bar appeared in her vision and decreased by twenty-five percent. Quinn's tired, battered body suddenly became energized in the same way she'd felt inside the simulator.

Cindy's face showed her surprise at her opponent's strength and speed when Quinn blocked the first series of blows she delivered.

Quinn raised her forearm faster than she'd ever moved before, blocking another combination attack.

She decided to return the favor.

Quinn swung the dagger, making the possessed girl dance backward. She barely avoided the slashing blow.

Cindy cocked her head to one side as if trying to gauge Quinn's speed and strength. Then the black eyes narrowed, and she charged forward again with a growl.

The next flurry of blows came so fast, Quinn only managed to block about half of them. The others left her bruised and battered. At least she managed to stay on her feet.

Quinn knew they couldn't get caught in a long battle down here. Deciding to try something desperate, she waited until the next round of attacks came at her and staggered back two steps, drawing Cindy with her and making the other woman think she had the advantage.

After the second step, Quinn used her back foot to push off and spring forward, ducking what might have been a killing blow to her head from the demon-possessed redhead.

As the clenched fist flew past her face, Quinn twisted and hacked down, both hands locked on the dagger's hilt.

Cindy howled in what sounded like a combination of anger and pain as the blessed dagger sliced through her wrist and cut off her hand. The magical blade hissed as it passed through the girl's forearm, and a few wisps of smoke came from the stump.

To Quinn's surprise, there was no blood. Instead, ichor the same color as Cindy's eyes oozed out of the end of the arm.

Quinn stared for a split second, then regained her composure and readied her defenses.

The other woman sneered at Quinn as she retreated a few steps. "I don't know how you can fight so strongly after the beating I gave you earlier, but I won't underestimate you again, girl."

Quinn laughed and shouted back at the woman, "Come back here, and I'll cut off the other one."

Cindy looked over her shoulder and then at Quinn. "Maybe next time. If you survive."

The woman quickly backed away, leaving Quinn alone with Clark.

He stood over a lifeless Fergus, pulling the sword from the center of the now-dead man's chest. Wisps of smoke came from the hole the sword left behind. Several other bodies writhed on the ground around him.

Beyond Clark, Quinn spotted Myles farther down the tunnel, his hands raised and his lips moving. Cindy had returned to his side.

Quinn grabbed Clark's shoulder and pointed at Myles. "He's getting ready to cast a spell."

Clark didn't even look down the tunnel, just shoved Quinn. "Quick, run!"

Quinn ran.

Clark was right behind her.

From behind them, a burst of electrical energy shot up the tunnel.

Quinn was sure she was about to be fried, but the bolts of lightning splashed harmlessly off an invisible wall mere inches behind her.

Even though the electricity didn't reach her, the hair on her head stood on end for a few seconds.

Ahead of them at the elevator doors stood Miranda, her arms splayed as if she was pushing against an invisible force. Rivulets of sweat ran down her face, and she trembled from the exertion.

Clark and Quinn raced up the tunnel to stand next to her, then looked back.

The electricity surged against the barrier as if trying to seek a way around it.

Quinn saw the elevator coming down the shaft toward them.

"Just hold it a few more seconds, Miranda. The elevator's almost here."

The woman didn't say anything but gave a tiny nod of understanding.

Clark pointed at Taylor. "Get her ready to run inside. I'll take care of Miranda."

Quinn nodded and moved to stand beside Taylor.

The other girl pointed down the tunnel at the display of magical energy and destruction. "What the hell is going on, Quinn? It's like Mr. Hickman is trying to kill us or something."

Quinn rolled her eyes. Sometimes Taylor was a little slow on the uptake. "I'll explain it to you later. Get in the elevator. Hurry."

Not waiting for the elevator doors to open fully, Quinn gave Taylor a shove and she stumbled into the corner of the car.

Quinn ran in behind her and reached for the control panel, waiting for Clark and Miranda.

He bolted into the elevator, carrying the sorceress. Her eyes were open, but she was listless in his arms.

"Close the doors. Now."

Quinn mashed the button that closed the doors, then Up, and the car started to move.

A split second after the car headed up the shaft, Miranda's barrier failed, and a blast of electrical energy slammed into the empty space beneath them.

The explosion below knocked all of them from their feet, but the elevator car continued upward while they struggled upright, ears ringing.

They'd made it.

CHAPTER TWENTY-FIVE

The elevator rose up to the basement level, and the doors slid open. Clark stepped out first, supporting Miranda with one of her arms across his shoulders.

He didn't get far.

A fist slammed into his head from the side, knocking him against the wall hard enough that Quinn heard the crack of bone as his shoulder impacted the concrete wall. Miranda fell in a daze to the floor outside the elevator.

"Clark," Quinn shouted.

A man stepped into her way, blocking her view of the injured hunter. The newcomer's eyes were as black as Cindy's.

It was Jared, the candidate from the earlier test group. He laughed at the horrified look on Quinn's face.

She recovered quickly.

Using the last of her earlier stamina boost, Quinn kicked out at Jared, catching him by surprise and sending him flying down the short hall.

"Taylor, find some way to wedge these doors open. We can't let the elevator close and return to the caves."

Quinn didn't wait to see if Taylor heard. She dove at the demon-possessed candidate, trying to get to him before he got back to his feet, as she drew from her stamina again.

Jared kicked with both legs, kipping up and landing on his feet as Quinn got there.

He reached for her, but Quinn's strength and speed were enhanced. She ducked under his swipe and rolled past him, coming back to her feet as she twisted and slashed at the back of his knees with the holy blade.

The dagger cut deep into one leg, buckling it. Jared almost fell over backward.

Once again, as with Cindy in the caves below, there was no blood as the blade came away, just thick black ooze from the edges of the wound.

Quinn bounced up to attack again, only to have to dodge as a pair of fists swung past the spot her face had been a split-second before.

Jared smiled as he fixed her with his black eyes. "Myles assured us the hunter clans were finished, yet here you are, trying to stop that which is inevitable."

"If it was so inevitable, why am I standing here, ready to keep fighting, while you can barely stand on that leg I slashed open?"

"You hunters were always cocky. I remember that from the last time I walked this plane."

"I wouldn't know about that. I'm a new breed of hunter, the kind who is going to put you all in your place once and for all."

"Oh, so you believe yourself to be the vaunted Chosen One of hunter legend?"

Quinn didn't know what that meant, but she did know she couldn't afford to stand here chatting with the demon.

Feinting toward where Clark lay crumpled against the wall, Quinn turned at the last instant and lunged, trying to skewer Jared with her dagger.

He laughed and batted it away with ease.

The blow almost knocked the weapon from her hand.

Jared sneered and said, "You think you can defeat us here on our own ground? It's only a matter of time until more of the brethren come to take you."

Before Quinn could think of an answer, Jared launched a series of attacks using both his hands and feet.

Only because his one leg was injured and didn't work was Quinn able to dodge the concentrated barrage.

As it was, he managed to connect with her right shoulder. Quinn felt something snap, and a surge of searing pain raced down her arm.

She wasn't sure what he'd broken, but something was wrong with her right arm now. It wouldn't move without waves of agony running through her shoulder.

Quinn tried to hide the severity of her injury and managed to slash out with the dagger as Jared dove at her again.

She connected with the dagger as she thrust it out in front of her. The point plunged in, sinking a good six inches into the center of Jared's chest. He stumbled, clutching at the hilt and wrenching it from her hand.

She started to shout in triumph, but to Quinn's amazement, he didn't die. Instead, he hissed in pain and wrapped his hand around the leather grip, pulling the dagger free.

Jared staggered, injured from the wound but not fatally, it appeared. He held up the dagger smeared with black ichor from the wound, pointed it at her, and snarled, "It'll take more than this to kill me. You're not a true hunter. I see that now. You're just a girl, a mere huntress."

Something slid across the floor, bumping against her feet. It was Clark's sword.

Clark called, "Have to use my holy blade."

"I thought mine was like yours," Quinn complained.

"The sword is special. Use it. It's the only thing that will kill him and free the host's soul."

She bent down and grabbed the sword, holding it in front of her to fend off the wounded man.

Unseen behind Jared, Taylor came out of the elevator. She helped Miranda up and pulled one of the sorceress' arms over her shoulder.

The elevator doors closed behind the women, and the car started back down.

Damn, Taylor must not have been able to wedge the door. Myles and the others would be coming up soon.

Quinn circled to the left until she stood between her companions and Jared, the sword at the ready in front of her.

She took stock of the situation. Clark was struggling to get up, but he was sorely injured. Taylor would be no help, and Miranda was done, too. If anyone was going to protect them and get them all out of here, it would have to be her.

She glanced at her stamina bar, which was still hovering in front of her. The color had changed; it was now dark amber. She'd kept drawing on it as she fought Jared, and it showed only about twenty percent remaining. She didn't have much time left before it ran out.

She didn't know what would happen if she drew it all the way down during a fight, but it wouldn't be good. Quinn didn't have a choice, though. She had to hurry up and defeat Jared so they could get out of there. The elevator would return in a few minutes.

"Taylor, help the others get out. I'll be right behind you."

Quinn didn't wait to see if they'd started moving, just charged in, leading with her sword. The plan was desperate, and she was only going to get one shot at this.

Without warning, Jared sprang forward to meet her charge.

She hadn't expected that response. She'd thought he would wait for her to come to him.

He swept the dagger in and used the blade to parry the tip of the sword as it came at him.

Quinn switched her attack at the last instant, her response a last act of desperation.

Instead of trying to hold the sword in position to skewer the demon, she let the force of the parry swing the sword wide as she dropped to the floor.

The dagger's follow-up stroke passed just above her head, close enough to part her hair. Quinn didn't see it. She'd used the sword's momentum to help spin on her knees, bringing the short sword around at Jared's exposed torso.

The blade bit deep, cutting through the ribs and all the way to his spine.

Jared's legs gave out beneath him and he collapsed to

the floor, black ichor oozing from the wound. He'd dropped the dagger and was clutching the huge gash in his chest.

Quinn stood and moved to hold the sword poised over him, ready to strike again. "Time to finish you, demon. I'm a huntress, all right, and this huntress is going to kill you."

"I cannot be so easily killed. I might feel pain, but if this body is destroyed, I will simply transfer to another already prepared nearby."

Quinn didn't wait for him to say anything else. She plunged the sword into his heart, twisting the blade in the wound before pulling it free.

Jared's shocked eyes stared up at her as the blackness faded from them. Then he was the innocent guy he'd been before all this. He gasped and tried to say something to the woman standing over him, sword in hand.

Quinn struggled to find words to explain what she'd done.

She never got the chance. Jared's now-human eyes lost focus, shifting away from her face to fix on the ceiling as they glazed over in death.

Quinn straightened up and began gasping. Her stamina status flashed red, a mere sliver of the bar remaining. She'd stopped drawing on the power bar in time, but she nearly collapsed as the enhanced strength and speed left her.

Suddenly, every part of her battered body flooded her brain with pain. Gasping for air as she pushed past the surges, Quinn limped down the short hall to the door leading back to the basement.

Taylor stood on the other side, staring wide-eyed

through the window. As Quinn approached, the other girl opened the door for her and held it to let her through.

Quinn stepped into the room. Clark stood nearby, cradling his crushed arm with his free hand. Miranda leaned against one of the stainless steel tables, nearly collapsing from exhaustion due to her magic expenditure.

"He's dead," Quinn said. "The elevator's on the way back up, so we need to get out of here."

Clark nodded. "Let's go, then. We've been here long enough."

He started toward the door to the long basement hallway. Taylor moved to help support Miranda as they followed Clark. Quinn considered the door behind them but decided she couldn't block it, so she limped after them as fast as she could.

They reached the stairs and headed up to the main level. Quinn was unsure where to go at that point, though.

"How did you two get in here?"

Miranda pointed to the double doors all the way down the long hall that led to the main entrance. "Clark and I came in the front, but we can't get out that way. We're both spent."

Quinn thought for a minute, then pointed up the hallway to the entrance to the testing wing. She'd remembered something from the first session in the VR system. "There's a side corridor just past the locker rooms. I think there's an exit sign pointing that way. It must lead to a door that opens somewhere at the back of the building."

Clark nodded, and the four of them started up the corridor.

Quinn held Clark's sword in her one good hand. It was

the only weapon they had left. She hoped they didn't end up in another fight on the way out.

Luckily, they encountered no one else. Everyone was either down in the caverns or had left for the night.

They entered the testing wing, and Quinn led them to the bend in the corridor near the locker rooms.

There it was.

The exit sign hung from the ceiling just where she remembered it.

They all shuffled toward the emergency exit, almost making it out of the building before an alarm sounded from the overhead speakers.

Myles had reached the basement and raised the alert.

"We need to get out *now*," Quinn said. "Hopefully the exit isn't locked down because of the alarm."

"We'll find out," Clark replied.

The sign on the said, *Emergency Exit Only. Alarm will sound when opened.*

Quinn laughed. "Don't need to worry about that, do we?"

She pushed the panic bar down, praying the door opened.

It did, and cool night air flowed in.

Clark started to push past her, but Quinn held him back with one arm. "Let me go first. I'll make sure the coast is clear."

"Be careful. Don't go far."

Quinn nodded as she opened the door all the way and stepped outside. She peered through the darkness to see if anyone was there. Then she remembered.

"Dammit, I need to see."

Instantly, the darkness was gone, shades of blue tinting everything. She scanned the area, looking both ways for trouble.

Alarms sounded from both inside and at the front of the building. Here in the back, though, things were relatively quiet.

A broad, grassy area stretched for a hundred yards or so to a tall stone wall.

Quinn gestured to the others. "Let's go."

The others came out, and Quinn turned toward the parking lot.

Clark shook his head. "We need to go back the way Miranda and I came in. You'll never get out the front gate. Too many guards."

"Which way, then?"

Clark pointed toward the stone wall across the field. "That way. My car's parked on the other side."

"Good, let's go." Quinn moved to help Taylor with Miranda, while Clark led the way.

At the wall, which was nearly eight feet tall, Quinn and Taylor worked together to lift Miranda to the top.

She reached the top, nodded down at them, and slipped out of sight as she dropped to the other side.

"You're next, Clark."

He stepped up, and Quinn boosted him up to the top. He grunted in pain as he let go of the injured arm to let it hang at his side. He had no choice. He had to use his good hand to get to the top.

Once there, he straddled the wall and reached down.

"Come on. We need to hurry before someone spots us from the building or drives by."

Taylor was pulled up first while Quinn boosted her.

Once her friend was over safely, Quinn took Clark's hand and pulled herself up and over.

From atop the wall, Clark pointed to a storage center across the road about fifty yards away. "My car is in the lot over there."

"Good," Quinn said. "Let's get out of here."

The other two had already started toward the storage center's lot, and Quinn and Clark hurried to catch up. Both Quinn and Clark reached for the driver's door.

Clark shot her a glance.

Quinn laughed. "You're in no condition to drive. Give me the keys."

"You've got a bum arm, too."

"Just give me the keys. I promise to be careful."

Clark actually chuckled and dug them from his pocket. "You should see yourself before you go criticizing me." He handed her the keys and went around to climb into the front passenger seat.

Quinn slid in, started the car, and turned to look at Taylor and Miranda. "Everyone in?"

They both nodded, and Quinn drove out of the lot into the early morning light.

CHAPTER TWENTY-SIX

Two days later, Quinn paced the floor in Clark's seedy little apartment. It barely had two rooms. There was a small kitchen area that also served as part of the living room, a tiny bathroom, and a single bedroom.

She turned and looked through the grimy window at the city street outside. "Why can't we go back and try to find the others?"

Clark laughed.

There was little humor in his face when Quinn spun to confront him. He held up a hand to forestall her response.

"Quinn, we're in no condition to do anything. Besides, they'll be expecting us. Until we gather more information and find additional help, we'll stay here."

He sat at the small dining table, his arm still in a sling. He'd insisted he didn't need a doctor or a hospital, claiming his enhanced hunter healing ability would take care of it in a few days.

Quinn couldn't argue with him. He moved the injured shoulder better today than yesterday, and she knew how fast her own injuries were healing, following their escape from VirSync.

Miranda chimed in to agree with the older hunter. "Clark's right. We have to stay put while we gather our strength. I've still not recovered from the other night. I overextended myself in ways I never thought I'd have to. It's going to take me at least a week to get back to normal."

Taylor looked up from her spot on the sagging couch next to Miranda. She'd been watching TV and mostly ignoring their ongoing discussions about what to do next. "I'd like to repeat my request to let Quinn and me go back to our apartment and get some more clothes. I'm tired of wearing a pair of Clark's sweatpants and t-shirts. I need a bra, at least."

Clark shook his head. "It's too dangerous. They're sure to be watching your place. You can never go back there. In fact, I need to reach out to some friends and see about getting you both new identities."

Taylor smiled. "Can I pick my new name? That would be fun, Quinn. We could pick something exotic and sexy, right?"

Quinn resisted the urge to roll her eyes. They'd uncovered a plot to take over the world and saved Taylor from demonic possession, and she was worried about what her new name might be.

"I'm not changing my name," Quinn said. "It's the only thing I have left from my parents. It ties me to them and to the legacy they tried to leave me."

"Does that mean you've decided to begin your training as a hunter?" Clark asked.

Quinn nodded. "I like the new things I can do. I want to find out how much more I'm capable of."

"It's not going to be easy, you know."

"Stop trying to dissuade me. I'm doing this. They're not going to stop. Myles and his cult of demon worshipers will continue their efforts to destroy the world as we know it. I have to train and learn so we can go back after them."

Miranda nodded. "We also need to figure out exactly how they're using that VR technology coupled with magic to send their unwitting assassins out to kill those who'd stand in their way."

Taylor laughed and raised her hand. "Oh, I can answer that. The breakthrough came when they figured out a new kind of computer-neural interface. They'd discovered a powerful new energy source, which I now know comes from the magical spells they use. The combination makes it possible to open up some sort of breach in space and time. That was how they got us to the city and back again."

The apartment's other three occupants stopped their conversation and stared at Taylor.

She noticed the awkward silence after a few seconds and twisted her head to find them all looking her way.

"What? It's not something I've ever seen before or fully understand, but I saw enough of the code before I was sent into the VR system each time to get the gist of what they were doing. I'd talked with Claire and Gary about it, and we compared notes. That's how I figured it out."

Clark leaned forward in his chair. "Taylor, that's great news. So you can replicate it and duplicate the system they're using to transport the candidates to their targets?"

Taylor shrugged. "I might be able to. I would need the

right equipment, and that doesn't take into account needing a way to magically energize it the way they did."

"I can probably do that," Miranda said. "We'd have to experiment to get it right. If you can recreate the proper computer programming, though, I should be able to feed you enough magical energy to make it work, at least in theory. We'd probably have to try a couple of different things to magnify my abilities, but I'm confident we can figure it out once we get the basic configuration right."

Clark nodded. "If we could do that, we might be able to stop some of their incursions." He stopped, and his expression changed as his eyes displayed a deep sadness. "This is what the clans would've provided for us in another time and place. The collective energy of all worked together and created a sort of strength in numbers and abilities was hard to overcome, at least until we were betrayed."

"What's to stop that from happening again?" Quinn asked.

"The clans are gone, Quinn. They've been gone for almost twenty years. We can't just resurrect them, can we?"

Quinn didn't answer, looked around the apartment. Taylor had stopped watching TV. Miranda smiled her way, and Clark just sat there and scowled at her like he always did.

It was then that Quinn understood what they needed to do. "Why can't we?"

"What can't we what?" Clark asked. "Why can't we resurrect the clans? They're all gone, Quinn. I've told you that."

"But they're not, Clark. The purges didn't succeed. I'm proof of that. You are, too. You said you might be my distant cousin or uncle or something. You and I are part of a clan."

"Quinn, a clan's a lot more than two people."

"Hear me out. You said there are others out there like us, scattered around the world. Here in Baltimore, it's not just you and me. We have Miranda, and Taylor, too."

"They're not hunters. She's a witch, and I don't know what Taylor is."

"Gee, thanks," Taylor said.

Quinn shook her head. "You don't understand. Yes, the old clans as you knew them are dead and gone, but you also said they'd stopped being as effective as they were in the old days. Maybe it's time for us to start a new type of hunter clan. One that has more than just old-school hunters."

Miranda gestured at the others. "You're proposing that the four of us become the seeds of a new hunter clan?"

"Why not? That's what Myles and the others have done. They adapted to modern times and new technologies, using it to accomplish their evil ends. Maybe the hunters need to do the same thing. We might be late to the game, but we're not out of it. Taylor's got mad coding skills, and we've all seen what Miranda can do when it's needed. All we need is a couple of badass hunters to go after the bad guys."

Clark started to answer, then stopped and stared at the table. He seemed to be considering what Quinn had said. She decided to stop talking and let it sink in.

After at least ten seconds of silence, Clark looked up. "I've been trying to do this alone for so long, I forgot what it was like to work with a team."

Quinn shook her head. "We're not a team, Uncle Clark. We're a clan—a new hunter clan forming here and now."

She caught the hint of a smile when she called him "Uncle." Quinn hadn't thought much about being related to him until now, but it felt right when she said it.

Miranda laughed. "What do you say, Uncle Clark? I'm in if you're in."

He shook his head, then chuckled. "Fine, I'll go along with this, but we're going to nip this Uncle Clark thing in the bud. Quinn, we might be related in some way, but if you want to start a new clan, then I become your Clan Master. Your sensei, to use a term you might understand better. Are you okay with that?"

Quinn beamed and nodded. "I can live with it."

Taylor bounced up from her seat on the couch. "So that's it? We're a clan now?"

Miranda smiled. "I guess we are, although I think we need to iron out some things about who's in charge of what."

"There has to be a leader," Clark said. "Someone has to be in charge. That's how this has to work."

"I'm not suggesting a democracy, Clark," Miranda answered. "But my experience with a coven is a sort of collective leadership based on each person's strengths. When it comes to hunter stuff and training Quinn, you are the one in charge. Since that's the primary role of a hunter clan, that makes you our clan leader. For the support stuff and creating this new hybrid tech-magic interface, though, Taylor and I will take the lead. Agreed?"

Clark nodded. "Agreed."

Quinn thought for a few seconds and then said, "Hey,

what's that make me, some sort of probie?"

Clark laughed. "That makes you something that hasn't existed in over twenty years."

"What's that?"

"A clan initiate, a hunter in training. This was your idea, Quinn. We all have our roles. This is yours. You have to agree to it, though. You have to say it aloud to make it official."

As Clark spoke, the amulet around Quinn's neck pulsed to match her heartbeat. She traced its outline beneath her shirt, feeling the faint vibrations through her fingertips. A memory came to her from the fight in the caverns, something demon-possessed Jared had called her. She smiled.

"I accept, but I'm not a hunter. I'm something better. I'm a huntress."

Clark nodded. "Very well." He got up and came over to her, laid his hand on her head, and said, "Welcome to the clan, Huntress Initiate Quinn Faust."

Quinn's eyes widened as the amulet flared with energy only she could feel.

It infused her with power, leaving her tingling from head to toe. At the same time, a woman's voice sounded in her head, one that was familiar somehow. It brought tears to her eyes.

Welcome, and well done, my daughter, my Quinn, my new huntress.

Quinn is just learning what it means to be a Huntress. Will she master her new skills and abilities in time to save her best friend? Find out in *Huntress Apprentice!*

HUNTRESS APPRENTICE

It's a fight just to survive. VR assassins and demonic forces lurk in the shadows in this hidden world. Doesn't help that there's something, or someone, else gunning for them too.

Can an apprentice Huntress, a grizzled veteran, a lone sorceress, and a tech witch find a way to stop a newer, even greater evil?

As Quinn finds her way with her new abilities, she and her new clan continue their work to counter the efforts of demons bent on invading our world.

Caught in an epic battle between the light and the dark as old as time, the Huntress and her team may only have one chance to save those she's sworn to protect.

Will it be enough?

Join Quinn and her friends as she continues to learn and explore what it means to be the Huntress, eventually taking their fight into the lair of an evil power they didn't expect.

Available now at Amazon and through Kindle Unlimited

JAMIE'S AUTHOR NOTES

NOVEMBER 26, 2019

As Thanksgiving approaches, I get pretty angsty about getting everything done that needs doing. It makes me pretty testy to be around. The thing is, I shouldn't be all tied up in a knot about things. My wife and I just got to be grandparents for the first time and I now understand the fun of that job. You get to play with them all you want and give them back for diaper changes.

I've chosen to be called Obi (short for Obi Wan) and yes, I plan on calling the grandkids padawans. Just another of the joys of being a fantasy and sci-fi author, I get to be quirky like that. I'm looking forward to this next chapter in my life.

This book, *Huntress Initiate*, represents another sort of birth for me. It's the birth of a new series. It's been a long time coming and is not just a result of my efforts. I also comes from the support of my wife, my mentor on the project Craig, and the thoughtful feedback of some awesome beta readers who helped me file away Quinn's rough edges.

Just like the new baby in our family, I plan on shepherding this project forward, raising it from a newborn book and series to wherever it will take us. Quinn has a lot on her plate and will have to work hard to make her life work out the way she wants. This Obi plans on being there to carry her when needed along the way through the Huntress Clan Saga.

If you want to follow along, I post occasional videos along with more frequent written posts about current projects on which I'm working and a bunch of other random fun, funny, and nerdy stuff about fantasy books of all sorts in my reader group on Facebook, Jamie's Fun Fantasy Readers. Look me up and join the fun.

Extreme Medical Services: Medical Care On The Fringes Of Humanity

Monsters, Paramedics, and Street Medicine

New paramedic Dean Flynn is fresh out of the academy.

Then he learns his patients aren't your normal 911 callers.

With patients that are vampires, werewolves, fairies and more, will Dean survive his first days on the new job?

Will his patients?

Come along now with Extreme Medical Services, a supernatural medical thrill-ride with the paramedics of Elk City by best-selling author and real-life paramedic Jamie Davis.

Jump on the ambulance with Dean, Brynne and the rest of the team.

Get the first book in this best-selling service for free at Amazon.com.

Extreme Medical Services Series (8 Urban Fantasy books)

Read book 1 - Extreme Medical Services

—

The Delivery Mage (5 Urban Fantasy books)

Book 1 - *Deliver or Die*

—

The Broken Throne Series (5 Urban Fantasy books)

Read book 1 - *The Charm Runner*

—

The Accidental Traveler LitRPG Trilogy

(with C.J. Davis)

Read book 1 - *The Accidental Thief*

—

Accidental Champion LitRPG Trilogy 2

(with C.J. Davis)

Read book 1 - *Accidental Duelist*

—

Sapiens Run (3 Dystopian Sci-fi books)

Book 1 - *Cyber's Change*

—

Eldara Sister Series (2 Historical Fantasy books)

Read book 1 - *The Nightingale's Angel*

CONNECT WITH THE AUTHOR

My author site is: https://jamiedavisbooks.com

My Facebook group is: https://facebook.com/groups/funfantasyreaders